P9-CQL-260

W McCord, John S
   Wyoming giant

DATE DUE			
NOV 1 9 1992			
JAN 4 1993			
FEB 1 1993			
FEB 2 0 1993			

Mynderse Library
31 Fall Street
Seneca Falls, NY 13148

The Baynes Clan:
Book Three

Wyoming Giant

The Baynes Clan:
Book Three

Wyoming Giant

John S. McCord

A DOUBLE D WESTERN
DOUBLEDAY
New York   London   Toronto   Sydney   Auckland

A Double D Western
PUBLISHED BY DOUBLEDAY
a division of Bantam Doubleday Dell Publishing Group, Inc.
666 Fifth Avenue, New York, New York 10103

A Double D Western, Doubleday,
and the portrayal of the letters DD
are trademarks of Doubleday, a division of
Bantam Doubleday Dell Publishing Group, Inc.

All of the characters in this book except
for certain historical figures are fictitious,
and any resemblance to actual persons, living or
dead, is purely coincidental.

Library of Congress Cataloging-in-Publication Data

McCord, John S.
Wyoming giant/John S. McCord. —1st ed.
p.   cm. — (A Double D western) (The Baynes Clan; bk. 3)
I. Title.   II. Series: McCord, John S.   Baynes Gang; bk. 3.
PS3563.C34439W96   1992
813'.54—dc20   92-5634
CIP

ISBN 0-385-41498-6
Copyright © 1992 by John S. McCord
All Rights Reserved
Printed in the United States of America
October 1992
First Edition

W

MYNDERSE LIBRARY
31 Fall Street
Seneca Falls, New York 13148

To Joan, and my favorite daughter, Merrie Lynn, and my favorite son, John.

The Baynes Clan:
Book Three

Wyoming Giant

PROLOGUE

THE LITTLEST THINGS can make a man uncomfortable. We are all, perhaps, more creatures of habit than we think. When I stepped off a train in New York, clothes wrinkled in the baggy fashion of 1869, both my pistols were tucked into my carpet-bag. I'd packed them into their holsters and rolled them in the belts I'd worn around my middle every day of the ten years since I was sixteen.

Being in a strange place had nothing to do with my anxiety. Traveling had come to be my way of living since that grim day six years ago when my mother died. A posse rode to our front porch the evening of that tragic day and pulled iron, determined to force me and my brothers at gunpoint to join the Confederate Army. They figured to burn the place too, I suppose to give an example to any others who hesitated to join the boys in gray.

All six of the men in that posse learned too late the hazard of trying to force my family to do anything against Pa's wishes. The so-called Baynes Clan, my pa and his three sons, left those men lying where they fell in the dusty front yard of the house where I was born. Pa judged traveling to be prudent after that, so we saw a lot of country.

About four years later, my pa went partners with a hard-eyed ex-Confederate officer named Joseph Thackery in a gold strike in Montana Territory. They got rich in no time at all. Pa and Thackery became inseparable friends, continued their partnership, and went into several kinds of businesses with their mining profits. But they still wore their guns.

My youngest brother, Ward, the one said to be an ice-cold, unfeeling gunfighter, fell for Thackery's pretty daughter. He won a wagon-load of money betting on himself in a horse race, married Kit Thackery, and went off to California. He built a fine ranch there, started breeding and training the best horses west of the Mississippi, and became the soul of respectability. But he still wore his gun.

My next-to-youngest brother, Milton, took offense at rumors of villainous crimes blamed on us after we left home. With the itchiest feet of us all and the habits of an Apache warrior in hostile country, he took the notion to return to Louisiana to clear our name.

He never made it. Instead, he ran into a fiery red-headed girl in Texas, lost his taste for traveling, and went into the cattle business, happy as a pig in warm mud. Milt looked handsome and civilized when I rode through. His wife cut his long hair and started him to wearing cloth instead of leather. But he still wore his gun.

Since my pa became a big, respectable businessman, and since both my brothers found wives and put down roots, only one member of the notorious Baynes Clan still floated on the wind.

I stood in a train station in New York, the oldest of the brothers at twenty-six, the tallest at four inches above six feet, the heaviest at 220 pounds, and the loneliest, still having found nobody to hog my covers at night.

And I couldn't keep my hands away from the empty places on each hip. A sheared sheep in midwinter would have felt more comfortable than did Luke Baynes without his guns. Probably, my wearing two instead of the usual one indicated my attitude about life. A man with a violent past grows hardened to it and anticipates a violent future. I put it from my mind and moved on. I was looking for a man.

ONE

THE YOUNG MAN seated at the desk managed somehow to look down his nose at me, a fine feat since I stood leaning over him.

"You have no appointment, sir. You can't see Mr. Lorane without an appointment."

"My uncle's lawyer sent a letter ahead of me. Mr. Lorane wrote back that he'd see me as soon as I could get to New York. I'm expected." I kept my voice low. Most folks pay more attention to a man if they have to lean forward to hear him. On the other hand, a quiet manner of speech can sometimes help a man avoid unwanted attention.

"I'll try to work you in next week, or perhaps the week after."

"I think you better tell Mr. Lorane I'm here and let him tell me to come back next week. I think you better do that. Is Mr. Lorane here?"

"That makes no difference, sir. He only sees people by appointment."

"Tell me, how far is it from that window to the street?"

With thinly disguised impatience, he said, "I'm sure I don't know. This office is on the third floor. I suppose it's thirty feet or so. Why?"

"Because it'll make good conversation this evening."

"Good conversation? I don't understand."

"It'll bring a laugh when I tell people I threw a man thirty feet today. They won't believe it till I admit most of it was straight down. That'll surely bring a chuckle."

He straightened in the wooden chair. "Are you threatening me, sir?"

"I'll give you a minute to ponder on it. Maybe you can puzzle it out by yourself."

I took about five steps across the luxurious carpet and took a seat in a chair beside the window. I leaned slightly to look out, like I was picking a good spot for him to land. The clerk came slowly to his feet and backed through the door beside his desk.

The instant the door shut behind him, I sprang up and crossed to the desk. All I needed was a quick glance behind it before I headed back to my chair. A moment later, a tall, distinguished man stepped through the door. He asked bluntly, "Did you threaten my clerk, sir?"

"Threaten?" I asked as I came to my feet. "That nice little man? My goodness."

He blinked in surprise as I kept unraveling to my full height. Men's eyes often flickered in this fashion when I came out of a chair. It's one of the little surprises a man of uncommon size can spring on folks.

His face relaxed into a faint smile, and I knew he recognized my little trick for what it was. Not the least diverted, he said, "Answer the question, sir."

"Are you Chance Lorane?"

"I am."

"Luke Baynes." I stuck out my hand.

He stiffened, but he took my hand.

"I believe you're the man who exchanged letters with Mr. Louis Flornoy of New Orleans. I have a letter expressing willingness to have me read law in this firm. I trust you are the Chance Lorane whose signature appears on this letter?"

He nodded, accepting the envelope I thrust at him.

"I also have a letter of introduction from Mr. Flornoy."

He nodded again, taking the second document. "Step into my office, Mr. Baynes. Louis's letters made you sound like the most interesting man in New Orleans."

Lorane turned but came to a sudden stop when he found his clerk still standing inches behind him in the doorway. He said, "Thank you for bringing Mr. Baynes to my attention, Mr. Sands. You exercised good judgment."

In his office with the door closed, Lorane seated himself behind a huge, cluttered desk and smiled. Eyes slightly narrowed, he said, "I think I'm already beginning to understand Louis's enthusiasm about you."

I waited for his gesture toward a chair before I took a seat. Louis Flornoy was a thorough teacher, not only of the law but of office decorum and everything else remotely connected with legal practice.

"How's that, sir?"

"I consider myself a clever lawyer, Mr. Baynes. Most others in this profession agree. Yet, I asked you a direct question twice, and you skillfully avoided answering it. Did you threaten my clerk?"

"That's your Mr. Sands, I believe?"

"Correct."

"He's surely a clever fellow, Mr. Lorane, but I fear he's overly sensitive. I merely attempted to clarify his thinking."

"How so?"

"I simply tried to help him examine the options available to him and the potential consequences of each."

"Did you threaten him?"

I faked a surprised expression and chuckled. "Only in a hypothetical and jesting manner, Mr. Lorane. Surely the little fellow didn't mistake my mildly humorous exaggeration for a serious threat of physical violence."

"You're twice his size. Nobody likes a bully, Mr. Baynes. I certainly don't."

"That must be a terrible burden for you, sir, having no friends in your chosen profession."

"I beg your pardon."

"I admit that I'm still very new to the legal business, sir, but Mr. Flornoy considered me a promising beginner. No offense, sir, but every good lawyer I've met so far has been the worst kind of bully. I don't believe I've met a single one who, given the least advantage over an opponent, doesn't turn into a domineering, sneering, nut-cutting bastard."

Lorane blinked several times, still sorting out my careful mixture of sharp words and gentle tone of voice. "Are you calling me a . . . ?"

"Oh no, sir," I interrupted. "I was expressing sympathy. Since you hate bullies so much, you must have very few friends in this profession. That's sad. Friends can be a comfort in hard times."

Lorane leaned back in his chair and steepled his hands on his chest, grinning at me. "Louis warned me that you had an odd sense of humor, but he said you were very quiet."

"He showed me his letter. I took that remark about being quiet to be a criticism which I have resolved to overcome. Thought I'd better show you right off that I can talk."

He nodded, still grinning. "Well, you pass the first test."

"No, sir. I believe that's the second test."

"I beg your pardon."

"I think little Mr. Sands was the first test."

"Oh, you do?"

"Yes, sir. I believe he knew I was coming. I think you put him up to trying to stall me, just to see what I'd do about it."

I put on an expression showing a glimmer of amusement, took a breath, and went on, "I think little Mr. Sands isn't about to let anybody bully his way in here. My guess is he's right good with that gun he has in the knee space of his desk."

Lorane snapped erect and stared at me for a second. Then

he leaned forward with narrowed eyes and said, "Well, I'll be damned."

I grinned and nodded agreeably. "Since the first day I started reading the law with Mr. Flornoy, I've found that's a common supposition about the fate of lawyers."

Chuckling, Lorane swept aside a drape behind his desk and pulled an ornate cord. Instantly, a tap came on the door. Lorane spoke without raising his voice. "Come in, Cotton."

When the door swung open, Sands surveyed the room. Then he stepped in and stopped, poker-faced, keeping a comfortable distance from me.

Lorane said flatly, "Close the door."

Sands heeled the door shut.

"He read you like an open book." Lorane didn't sound happy.

"Yes, sir. I don't know why, but I felt he did."

Lorane turned to me. "Mr. Luke Baynes, may I introduce Mr. Roland Sands."

I stood and offered my hand. He took it firmly, his eyes meeting mine briefly with a chilling emptiness of expression.

Lorane asked, "Do we have any appointments this afternoon?"

Sands dropped my hand. "No, sir."

"Good. Latch the front door and put the closed sign on it. Then come back in here."

Sands reappeared in seconds and Lorane waved a hand at the two chairs in front of his desk. He said flatly, "We call Mr. Sands 'Cotton' around the office when clients aren't present. What shall we call you, Mr. Baynes?"

"Everybody calls me Luke."

"Fine. It's time for straight talk. I accepted you to read law with this firm for two reasons. First, anyone who gets such a high recommendation from Louis Flornoy must be exceptional. He's inclined neither toward exaggeration nor to florid praise. Second, there are many cases in New York, especially since the war, where lawyers are well advised to be on their guard. We have to deal with some of the, er, rougher elements in this great city."

"On guard? You expect trouble?" I asked.

"Almost routinely," he responded. "That's why Cotton isn't what he seems. He's a clerk, reads law himself at every opportunity, but most of all, he guards these premises and serves as an escort at times."

"You picked him because he's an unlikely-looking body-guard."

Lorane nodded. "Precisely. It would not be dignified to have a rough-looking person around this office. However, I believe him to be the best pistol shot in New York." He cleared his throat softly and added, "Also, Cotton is known to the rougher element. Few of them are eager to cross him. And finally, he feels he has a special reason to look out for us."

Lorane continued, "He had difficulty finding work after the war and got himself involved in a few, um, questionable activities which are best forgotten. However, a couple of waterfront toughs mistook his diffident manner for weakness and attempted to abuse his sister. He shot them both on the spot, promptly and efficiently. This firm defended him in court."

I asked, *"Pro bono publico?"*

"Yes, for the public good. Without fee."

"Why do I need to know this?"

"Because you and Cotton will work together. We have added you to the firm for two reasons. One, you come highly recommended. Two, your background indicates that you should be able to defend yourself better than some of the rest of us."

"My, my," I said mildly. "Officers of the court needing bodyguards in the settled and tame east? What a shock to my tender sensibilities."

Sands grinned for the first time, but Lorane made a sour mouth and said, "We've gone to great expense and effort to train Cotton to look like a harmless clerk. You weren't fooled. Why?"

I shrugged. "Ask him to wear dark spectacles."

Lorane leaned forward and asked, "Spectacles? Whatever for?"

"He's got the same look around his eyes as my youngest brother, Ward."

Lorane asked sharply, "What look?"

"Hard to say. Like my brother, Cotton is probably a surprise to the unwary. Pa said that about Ward years ago."

Cotton Sands didn't change expression, but something about him seemed to relax. He said, "I think I'd like your brother."

"Sure you would," I responded quickly. "Everybody does." I paused. "Except, maybe, the eleven surprised and unwary men he's killed."

I brushed a fleck of dust off my sleeve and waited a couple of seconds before I finished the way Ward would have. "Not counting Indians."

Then I turned to Chance Lorane and said, "I guess Cotton's pa taught him like our pa taught us. When somebody needs shooting, promptness and efficiency stand to be admired. Pa despised men who put off their chores or did sloppy work."

TWO

A BIRDLIKE WOMAN eyed me shrewdly from an ancient rocking chair. With her scanty white hair and lined face, she looked old enough to have danced with Julius Caesar.

The woman who'd answered the door and ushered me in spoke softly, "This is Mr. Baynes, Mother Belle."

Mother Belle dropped her eyelids briefly in response. Her gaze drifted to the serving woman, who turned to me. "Tea?"

I shook my head. She took my hat and backed out the door. "I'll get back to my cooking then."

The old woman gestured with one finger of a hand covered by a lacy, fingerless glove, and her gaze slid toward another rocker. I hesitated. The spindly chair appeared older than its owner and didn't look like it would hold my weight.

"Maybe I should just stand, ma'am, if you don't mind."

When she spoke, her voice was husky, seductive as a flirtatious woman a third her age. "When I suggest that you sit, Mr. Baynes, you sit. Since the day my husband built this house for me, nobody argues with me under this roof."

Trying to make myself as light as I could, I eased into the ancient chair about one pound at a time.

"Relax, Mr. Baynes. I picked everything in this house for a big man's comfort, and Mr. Belle paid for it like a big man, without sniveling. Quality ages, but it doesn't get flimsy."

"Yes, ma'am."

"You come recommended by Mr. Lorane, so I suppose he explained the rules. You understand there will be no female guests allowed other than those in residence?"

"Females aren't given to following me around, ma'am."

"You know that I accept only recommended guests?"

I shrugged.

"Don't be cavalier with me, Mr. Baynes. Did Chance Lorane explain our arrangement?"

Her tone had switched from seductive to tart. I didn't enjoy being addressed like a slow-witted schoolboy, so I had to force a soft voice for my answer. "People who stay here never use this address. Mail and other messages should be directed to Mr. Lorane's office. People here never talk about each other or even mention the names of the other guests."

I continued, "Anybody inside this house is safer than in a bank vault. Your servants are the best paid in the city. They are quiet, courteous, alert, discreet, and well armed. Your rates are outrageous, but I'm not to worry, since he's paying my rent. Mr. Lorane said your husband was the biggest grafter and most dangerous man in New York for over forty years."

She nodded and smiled. "Chance knew my husband well. He took over Mr. Belle's practice upon his death. Unfortunately, my husband's talents were appreciated by only a few associates. Mr. Lorane has been thorough, and it seems you understand the rules. I'll have Courtney show you to your suite."

She rang a tiny bell. The serving woman appeared quickly. "Take Mr. Baynes to his suite, Courtney."

Courtney turned to me. "This way, sir. You'll be on the second floor with Mr. Sands." She led the way.

I glanced toward the front door where I'd dropped my bag. She said, "Joseph took that upstairs."

"Joseph?"

"My man." She led me up the stairs and down a carpeted hall brightened from both ends by wide, floor-to-ceiling windows. When she opened a door and led the way inside, I walked into a sitting room like nothing I'd ever seen. The Queen of England probably had no better.

She opened another door leading to a bedroom big enough to stable twenty horses. "Me and Joseph look after everything. You don't want something touched, you got something private, you tell me about it right now."

Slowly, I said, "Well, I can't think of anything I don't want you to touch except maybe . . ."

"Most gentlemen come here armed. Joseph probably put one of your pistols in that little table by the bed and, if you have another, it'll be in that little table by the door. The holster belt will be hanging in the closet yonder. If you find better places for them, that'll be fine. Joseph puts things where he thinks you'll like them, easy to hand."

"I'd like to look in on Mr. Sands."

"His suite's on the other side of the hall. I'll ask Mr. Sands if he's receiving visitors."

"Thank you."

She closed my door firmly before she took the few steps down the hallway. I listened with all my might, but all I heard was a couple of light taps and a few words spoken too softly to make them out. A few seconds later, Courtney paused outside my door, said quietly, "Mr. Sands will receive you in ten minutes," and walked silently away on the thick carpet.

Feeling like a kid caught snooping, I turned away from the door glad she couldn't see my embarrassment through solid oak. A quick check revealed that most of my meager belongings were hung neatly in a huge, meticulously polished chifforobe, with the remainder folded carefully into its two drawers. The invisible Joseph moved fast. I pulled open the drawer in the bedside table. The loads in my .44 had not been disturbed, but the barrel and cylinder showed a light sheen of fresh oil. Incredible man, Joseph.

At my rap, Cotton Sands opened his door and greeted me with a hard grin. "Accommodations satisfactory?"

Shutting the door, I answered, "Never trust a roof till after a hard rain."

"Drink?"

"Don't use it much."

"Have a seat. How do you like New York so far?"

"Haven't tasted enough of it yet. Don't know whether to swallow or spit. What am I getting into here, Cotton?"

He shrugged. "Relax. Somebody shot at Chance Lorane a few years back, and he had a couple of witnesses disappear. It made him a fanatic about caution. I wouldn't let it worry me. It's just a habit with him."

"What does a man do around here besides work?"

"What do you like?"

"I like to ride. I'm used to open spaces. I grew up near New Orleans, but I knew my way around there, so I didn't feel trapped by a bunch of buildings."

Cotton nodded. "We'll get you a membership in all the best clubs. Mr. Lorane insists we meet as many people as we can. People prefer to hire a lawyer they know rather than a stranger. Riding clubs, shooting clubs, athletic clubs, we join them all. We get to know the best-dressed criminals in the city by their first names. Cigar?"

I shook my head. "Never picked up the habit."

"Tell me, why did you come all the way to New York? Don't they have legal problems to solve in New Orleans?"

"Plenty, but most of the work they do in Louisiana is based on the Napoleonic Code. Louis Flornoy thought I needed to practice with a good man under English common law."

He nodded. "That's smart. Mr. Lorane's intrigued with you. He says you have almost no formal schooling."

"Never felt that hurt me. My mother taught me and my brothers better and smarter than what I hear most folks get in schools. In fact, I've come to the opinion that most schools and churches teach people dumb things."

A woman's voice came from behind me. "Are you against religion, sir?"

I came to my feet. Framed in the doorway stood the most spectacularly beautiful woman I'd ever seen. Tall, strongly built, with hair so light it appeared almost white, she had one brow cocked in question.

Cotton said, "Helen, may I present Mr. Luke Baynes. Mr. Baynes, this is Miss Helen Sands, my sister."

She curtsied, making her graceful move an act of mockery.

"No offense intended, ma'am. It's wise to take care when criticizing folks who have good intentions, and people in schools and churches certainly have that. But they teach children things they can't use, it seems to me."

"Such as, Mr. Baynes?"

"Perhaps you'd like to take a seat, ma'am, now that you can hear better than you could from the next room."

She flushed. "I do believe I've been reprimanded for eavesdropping."

I lifted a chair into position close to where Cotton and I had been seated. She took the hint and sat down.

"The point I wanted to make, ma'am, had to do with churches and schools spending a lot of time teaching children to be good and to avoid evil. That doesn't help much in the adult world, doesn't help solve most grown-up problems."

"What would you suggest, Mr. Baynes? Please do share with us the Luke Baynes version of wisdom." She put the fingers of one hand softly against her cheek, as if to draw away the heat of the angry blush still coloring her features.

Cotton and I sat down facing her. "I'd suggest children be taught to look down the road and consider the consequences of what they do. They should be taught to choose the best action to take based on the consequences they want."

"I'm afraid you've lost me, sir." Helen Sands blinked at me with the blank look of an empty-headed southern belle. On her, that expression was as calculated to irritate as a man's turning his back.

"I'll try to simplify, ma'am," I said, returning the insult by pretending I believed her blank expression to be genuine. "Which is more important, tact or truth?"

She snapped, "Truth, of course."

"Always?"

"Are you setting a trap?"

"Certainly, ma'am."

"Then spring it, by all means."

"All right. Let's say your brother gives you a gift, and he's beaming with pride. You hate the gift. Naturally, you drop it into the wastebasket at once and tell him you wish he'd bought something other than that horrid trash."

She stared at me.

"I think you'd shove truth aside. You'd care more about Cotton's feelings than you'd care about the truth. You'd lie. To tell the truth would be mean. You aren't mean, are you?"

Her eyes were dark brown, like bittersweet chocolate. We stared at each other for a few seconds until Cotton cleared his throat uneasily. Then Helen turned to him and said calmly, "Seat me beside Mr. Baynes this evening, Cotton. He's the first interesting man I've met since we moved here." Her gaze dropped and she said, "I may have walked a bit slowly getting to the doorway to reveal myself. I didn't mean to eavesdrop."

I gave her my best beaming grin, the one my mother used to claim could melt butter. "I'd like to escort you to dinner, if I may have the honor, ma'am. I'll sit by you if I have to hit somebody on the head with a spoon to empty a chair."

Only a few rarely beautiful women can smile like a break in the clouds on a stormy day. A smile that can light the world is a priceless and wonderful gift.

THREE

THE PEELING SIGN above the door identified the Rolled Sail pub. The grimy building crouched at the end of a narrow alley near the waterfront. The establishment boasted the coldest beer and the spiciest gumbo north of Louisiana.

The heavy furnishings showed scars collected when customers consist mostly of beached sailors. Our expensive, tailored clothing could hardly have attracted more attention if our hats had been on fire, but Cotton spoke to several men by name and seemed unaware of the curious stares from others.

He ordered a bowl of gumbo and finished it only shortly after I finished the two bowls I ordered. My brothers often teased me about how fast I could eat. Mostly, I got it done faster than others because they spent time talking, and I seldom spoke much when food lay in front of me. Cotton shoved his empty bowl away impatiently and said, "You won another one this morning. How do you do it?"

I shrugged. "I had a year reading law in New Orleans before I came up here."

"You've made fools of some of the best lawyers in this town. Still, they haven't caught on. Everybody talks about the big country boy who's come to town and got lucky."

"They're right."

"Nonsense. You've been here three months and haven't lost a case. That's not luck. I should have suspected something when you passed your bar exam after only a week of study. One week! Fantastic. I thought Chance bought you a good score."

He looked sour when I showed surprise. "Don't give me that simple, confounded look. You know scores can be bought if you know how, and knowing things like that is Chance Lorane's pride and joy. Besides, you only work about half of every day unless you're in court. Then you disappear."

I shrugged again. "I go to the gym for a couple of hours most every day. I ride for about an hour. Then I go home to read and think. I told Chance I'd just as soon try to prepare a case in an iron foundry as in that office. I get restless sitting around too much, so I spar with a couple of guys once in a while, wrestle once in a while, run some. You have some good foot racers around here. I like those fellows."

"Helen says Courtney told her your light is on till late most every night."

"I don't need as much sleep as a rake like you."

Cotton leaned forward. "I like you, Luke, but I'm tempted to kick you sometimes. I hate it when you pull your country

boy act on me, because you fooled me with it. Helen warned
me, but I didn't listen."

"Your sister warned you about me? Why?"

"She said you tricked her. You made a few sharp-edged
remarks as soon as you were introduced, got her riled up,
caught her attention. Then you became the admiring gen-
tleman, hanging on her every word. She didn't even realize
what happened until she thought about it later. Helen says
you manipulate people. You find out all about them without
telling anything about yourself."

"She ought to be used to tongue-tied men around her."

Cotton rolled his eyes. "Poor Luke, just a stumbling, awkward oaf."

"All right, Cotton." I leaned forward and spoke slowly.
"You're a good friend. I'll tell you how it's done, how to be a
good lawyer or anything else you want to be. First, know
yourself. I come from a family that rides on the edge of the
devil's blade. There's a wild streak in my blood. If I don't
work it out, ride for miles, or do something to sweat it out
most every day, I get restless. That's a bad thing for my kind. I
have two brothers. Both of them catch fire quicker than a cat
can blink. We're a respectable family, but it's in us to be violent men. So that's the first thing. Do what you need to do to
have a cool mind. Got it?"

When he nodded slowly, I went on. "Next, this business of
being a lawyer is almost too easy to be fun. I've nearly memo-
rized Blackstone. All a man needs to do that is to be snowed in
a couple of winters with nothing else to read. I've read the
Bible through more than three times. There's wisdom in that
Holy Book, and it's meant to be used. When you quote scrip-
ture, juries pay close attention, and they should.

"I spent a lot of time out west. Out there, trials are the best
entertainment most folks have, serious drama. I've ridden two
hundred miles to watch a trial. I figured I could be a good

lawyer because I've seen so many bad ones. Most lawyers can't empty a boot without puzzling for an hour."

Cotton's eyes, wider than usual, stayed fixed on my face.

"Finally, you need to learn how to get people to talk. Some you joke with, some you scare, some you sympathize with, and some you treat with contempt, as if nothing they know matters anyway. Few men keep still if you find the right handle to pull. Me too. You just pulled my handle."

He squared his shoulders and flexed his fingers. "Thought you were going to come over the table at me for a minute."

When I lifted a hand in apology, he clapped his hands and laughed. "By golly, I've got it!"

"Got what?"

"You said it yourself. You've got to find the right handle to make a man talk, and I just found yours." He put on a smug expression. "Never fear, your secret is safe with me."

"What secret?"

"Your handle."

"All right, Mr. Lawyer. What's my handle?"

"Helen."

"What's she got to do with anything?"

"The minute I mentioned she said you manipulate people, you fired right up. You took that as a criticism. Your eyes sparked and smoke rings blew out your ears."

"She probably didn't mean anything unkind. Your sister's an amiable woman. She seems to take an interest in the law. Seems a strange thing for a woman to occupy herself with."

"Maybe that's why she's taken such an interest in you."

Heat rushed to my face, and I wondered if it showed. Likely it didn't. My dark skin offered some advantages. Caught by surprise, I retreated into my lifetime habit—if I didn't know what to say, I said nothing. Silence always outshines blurting out something dumb.

Two burly men shouldered their way to the bar, ignoring grunts of protest from those being shoved aside. One looked over his shoulder, caught my eye, and gave me a derisive smirk.

Cotton went on when I gave no answer. "She said you acted contemptuous of her at first, acted like all women are dumb. That attitude from men always makes her blazing mad. Then you started talking about interesting things and listened when she answered, really listened. That made her feel smart, like an exception to your low opinion of women."

I hid the heavy glass pepper shaker by cupping both hands around it and unscrewed the top with idle rubbing motions of one thumb.

The man at the bar who'd given me the insolent smirk spoke to his friend. Both turned, leaned their backs to the bar, and looked our way.

"Might be some trouble coming, Cotton." I eased my chair back a few inches.

He shrugged, pulled a big silk handkerchief from his pocket, and reached for the salt shaker. "Must be strangers. The bartender and several of the men in this bar know me. How many?"

"Two."

"Pick your man, country rube. I'll entertain the other."

When I glanced up again, the two smirking men swaggered from the bar toward us. They split to stand on both sides of our table between Cotton and me. The one who first caught my eye leaned down, fists on the table, and said, "You fancy boys sit somewhere else. We want this table."

I could tell he was set to hit me as soon as I came out of my chair, so I gave him the shakerful of black pepper before standing up. As I rose, I swung a backhanded blow at his friend, catching him squarely in the mouth with the heel of my fist and the base of the empty pepper shaker in my hand. Knocked back a step, he froze in wide-eyed surprise for a split second. Cotton, instantly on his feet, took a step forward, and

I saw a flash of white, heard a vicious crunch, and the man dropped.

Pepper Face blindly clawed at his eyes, gagging and spitting. I knocked his hands away and slapped him. His butt hit the floor with such a thump the tables jumped, and I heard the oddly pleasing pop and tinkle of falling glasses behind the bar. The sound of glass breaking always brought a grin to my face. There's just something about the music of breaking glass that sounds like fun.

A wondering voice said, "Just slapped him! Did you see that? Just slapped him and knocked him on his backside."

Pepper Face crawled away till his head bumped blindly against the bar. Still pawing at his eyes, he pleaded, "Somebody get some water. I'm burnin' up. I'm going blind."

The bartender lifted a bucket and looked a question at me. When I nodded he carried the bucket around the bar and flipped water at the choking, gasping man's face.

"Tell them they can have our table. We're leaving."

In a fine Irish brogue, the bartender said, "That's polite of ye, sor. You gentlemen come again."

Cotton carefully eyed the man he'd downed, a man now lying peacefully on his back with blood leaking from a bruised temple. Satisfied, he unloaded the salt shaker from his big handkerchief. He'd put the shaker in the center, lifted the corners and held them together. He'd used the shaker like a sap in that big square of silk, a weapon he'd made for himself in about two seconds. That explained the flicker of white.

Cotton and I stepped out the front door into the bright afternoon, and he asked, "How'd you knock him down with just a slap? Something hid in your hand?"

I took a deep breath and felt good. I stretched my arms up high and spread my fingers. As heavily callused as my hands were from long hours swinging a pick, I still felt the burn and tingle from the slap. "This life is fun, isn't it, Cotton? It's too good to pass up even a single minute of it. Nothing like a little scuffle to settle a good lunch."

"You going to answer my question?"

"That was a New Orleans slap, Cotton. Most people slap with the palm of the hand, maybe only the fingers. But if you really want to confound somebody, you hit with the heel of the hand. You can hit almost as hard that way as with your fist, but it humiliates and scares a man when you stagger him or knock him down with an open hand."

He chuckled. "So simple if you know how, and if you're big and strong as a mule."

"Yeah, simple as a salt shaker in a big handkerchief."

Cotton nodded and smoothed his coat. "In the future, big rube, don't be hitting my man. You knocked him back a step and almost made me miss. Don't hog the fun."

"No offense intended."

Carefully folding his handkerchief, Cotton said, "None taken. I just placed him, the one you slapped down. He seemed familiar, and I remember now where I saw him before. That was Sailor Dan O'Dell."

I shrugged.

"Don't take this lightly, rube. You just slapped down a popular up-and-coming prizefighter. He used to be a sailor, but he's been making so much money in the ring he stopped going to sea. I bet you'll hear from him again."

FOUR

MY PLAN to spend a year in New York hadn't included buying a couple of leather-covered cedar trunks and filling them full of overpriced new clothes. Nor had I planned to buy an expensive horse and memberships in exclusive clubs. Chance Lorane provided my room and board but paid me nothing.

I knew he was being generous even at that. Many aspiring lawyers in New York would be eager to pay him for the privilege of reading law in his prestigious office. Still, I'd spent more in the three months I'd been in New York than I'd planned to spend in a year.

Otherwise, I'd probably have laughed at the proposition John Morrissey offered the day after the incident in the Rolled Sail. Cotton escorted him into my office, introduced him, and backed out, closing the door. Morrissey, a big man with an engaging grin, held our handshake for an extra moment, twisted my wrist gently, and ran the fingers of his left hand across the back of my right. When he released me, he said, "Pleasure to meet you, Mr. Baynes. Would you make a fist for me, please?"

Puzzled, I did so, and he said, "Nice. Knuckles square off nice, the bones feel heavy and sound, and I find no knots or lumps from prior breaks. Few men have a natural ability to hit, and fewer have hands that can take the punishment. Maybe we can make some money together if you're a sporting man."

I motioned toward a chair, and he took a seat.

"You need a lawyer with good hands, Mr. Morrissey?"

He chuckled. "The lads have been talking about you, Baynes. They say you're good with your dukes. I hear you spiced Sailor O'Dell's lunch yesterday and slapped him flat."

"I had a brush with a fellow called Sailor O'Dell."

"How'd you like to try him without a handful of pepper?"

I shrugged.

"My man at the gym says you handle yourself better than any he's seen lately. You've been sparring with some good ones, or didn't you know that?"

"Who's your man?"

"John C. Keenan. Keenan was the man I beat to win the heavyweight championship back in 1858. When I retired, he became the champ again until Tom King beat him in 1863. He retired after that, but he keeps his eyes open. He thinks you can beat Sailor. If you can, there's a bit of money in it."

"How much?"

"Not so fast, lad. First, we'll go out of town for a little match or two to see how you do. Then we'll know more about our chances. Sailor's undefeated. There should be plenty of lads willing to bet on him against an unknown like you, if we keep you unknown until the right time."

He leaned forward to tap a finger on my desk. "The prize money for the little matches I have in mind will be about a hundred dollars or maybe a wee bit more. But if you bet on yourself and win, you can make a nice stake in a hurry."

"I'm not a gambling man, Mr. Morrissey." Even as I said it, I felt myself getting interested. Not being a man much troubled by modesty, I figured I'd earned the right to feel a bit cocky.

I'd had half a dozen matches with well-regarded pugilists in New Orleans before my family left our home in Louisiana. After we left, we explored most of the country that lay west of the Mississippi River and north of Mexico City.

Just about every town of any size we rode into had its proud man or two who owned what he thought was a fast horse.

Ward, my youngest brother, had a pet horse that outran them all and took their money. And plenty of towns had at least one man who thought he could whip anybody who only had two fists. If somebody wanted to see a show enough to put up prize money, I got interested. I never failed to ride out of town with that prize money. I guess I'd met about twenty and beat them all.

Each had some flaw which let me wallop them with little effort. Some were quick but couldn't hit with enough power to gain my respect. Others would have been troublesome if they'd kept themselves fit, but they spent too much time in saloons drinking with admirers. I'd met several who weren't boxers at all. They were brawlers who preferred to grapple and break an arm or gouge out an eye. Nobody paid attention to rules, if they'd ever heard of any.

In addition, many's the time I prevented my youngest brother from killing local fools. Usually all it took was for me to step in and deliver a New Orleans slap, put the fellow down, and then stand on his gun hand. Somehow that seemed to improve the thinking process of most of those boys. Other times it turned into an interesting scuffle for a few minutes.

We'd ride in and some ignorant fellow would try to pick an argument. They never picked on me or Milt, who seemed almost able to make himself invisible. Ward seemed to draw trouble. When challenged, he would turn and look his tormentor in the eye. The smart ones backed away fast. The dumb ones died if Milt or I couldn't intervene in time. Ward could get a handgun into action as fast, and had as little patience with fools, as anyone I ever saw. I always figured a good-natured whipping from Milt or me was better than getting shot by Ward.

I'd had opportunity to learn most every trick that could be pulled. And I'd learned that I had advantages. Few were as strong as I, and I'd met none with my endurance. Most times, when I hit a man solidly with either hand, he fell down and pondered the wisdom of getting up. I'd never had an opponent match my quickness. In fact, most big men paid little mind to footwork and speed of hand, depending on power alone.

Most of all, I'd given a lot of study to defense. There are two sides to boxing talent. One is to hit the other man effectively. The other is to avoid getting hit. No boxer can completely avoid being hit, so I'd caught many a well-delivered blow, but I had an iron jaw and skin like bull hide. I'd never been cut or knocked down. The absence of scars misled people, causing them to believe I had little experience.

The idea of picking up a few easy dollars had great appeal. New York fighters wouldn't be different from those in New Orleans, Los Angeles, Denver, or anywhere else I'd been.

All of this ran through my head in about two seconds while Morrissey grinned in my face, eyeing me shrewdly.

"What's your proposition, Mr. Morrissey?"

His grin widened. "You have the look of a man afraid of nothing. I was sure you'd take an interest. The deal is this. I arrange the bouts and see that prize money is put up, hard cash money in hand, no promises or IOU's. If you win, you keep the prize money. If you lose, you get nothing."

He paused a moment as if expecting me to speak. When I didn't, he went on. "I'll arrange a few contests against run-of-the-mill chumps, just to see how much you still need to learn. I won't send you up against anybody I don't figure you can handle if you try hard enough. How's that?"

"When do we start?"

He came to his feet. "I consider myself a judge of men, and I figured there'd be no dallying around, no hemming and hawing from the likes of you. How about tomorrow?"

"Where?"

"Don't worry about that. We have to travel, but it isn't far. I'll pick you up at noon. Where do you live?"

"Pick me up right here."

"As you like, lad."

"I'd like to take a friend with me."

"And who might that be?"

"Roland Sands, the man who brought you in here."

He nodded. "Bring him along if you like."

I escorted him out of my office and across the lobby. As soon as the front door closed behind him, I looked at Cotton and jerked my head toward my office. He followed me in, shut the door, and leaned against it. "Chance will grill you about this, Rube. You better have some good answers."

"Why?"

"Do you know who John Morrissey is?"

"Nope."

"Well, let's see. He's a former heavyweight boxing champion, and he's big in Tammany Hall."

When I didn't respond, Cotton added, "That's the political outfit that runs everything in New York."

I still made no response. Playing dumb, I'd found, was a good way to learn what others know. Playing smart, acting like you know it all, irritates people, and they stop talking. Cotton opened the door and scanned the empty lobby. He closed it again and said slowly, "That's the *crooked* political machine that runs everything in New York City. Morrissey owns a gambling house here in New York and another in Saratoga Springs. He owns a string of race horses. Oh, yeah, one other little thing. He's one of Chance's biggest clients. What did he want with you?"

"Offered to be my manager. He wants to arrange a few prizefights."

"You're not going to do that are you? Have you ever seen a prizefight?"

I nodded solemnly. "I've seen a few."

"You could get hurt. Why would you want to do a dangerous thing like that? You aren't that needful for money, are you?"

"Not really, I guess, but I'm running a little short."

Cotton said slowly, "I have the feeling you were about to say more. It's not the money, is it? It's something else."

"Yeah, I guess so."

"What is it?"

"Meanness."

"I beg your pardon."

"Meanness. I told you it runs in my family."

He narrowed his eyes and waited.

Finally, I told him the rest of it. "Cotton, there's a challenge to it, a thrill. When you get into that ring, you can't depend on anybody but yourself. There's no getting away from it, no dodging, no hiding. Nobody can help you. Nothing's left for you but to use all you've got. It's the greatest feeling in the world to have your hand raised in victory."

Cotton gave me a twisted grin. "The only way to win is to beat hell out of the other guy."

I gave him an exaggerated wink. "That's why I take to it. I never met a man in the ring I liked. All of them take me for a big, dumb rube. They can't wait to punish me, to tear me up, to smash me to a pulp. I like to see their faces when they go down. It's one of life's great pleasures to thump a bully."

"How soon are you going to do this?"

"Tomorrow. I told Morrissey you'd be going with me. I need you to watch a few things for me."

"Like what?"

"You need to carry a gallon jug of water and keep it in your hands through the whole fight. If you let anybody put anything in my water, I'll shoot you. You'll need a sponge, a couple of clean towels, a small bucket, and a few other things. Don't worry about it. I'll get the things I need and put them in a bag. Your job is to guard the bag."

"You think Chance will let both of us leave the office at the same time?"

"Yup."

"What makes you so sure?"

"You were the one who said Morrissey was a big client. I'll bet you two bits that Chance already knows about it. Bet?"

"Nope. I'll pass."

That evening at dinner, Helen leaned close and said softly, "Cotton told me what you plan to do tomorrow. I thought you were smarter than that."

I answered with a grin. "I bet this is the first time you've ever been wrong. Life is full of disappointments."

She gave me a look that would have killed a goat or a small horse, jumped up, and walked out, leaving half her meal untouched. When I looked Cotton's way, he pretended to be fascinated with his plate, never looked up once.

FIVE

As soon as I stepped into the carriage, I said, "I'll fight under the name Rube Cross today. Understood?"

Morrissey nodded and jerked a thumb toward a dark, greasy-eyed man who occupied the fourth seat, looking like the sort who lurked forever in dimly lit alleys. The man's glance slid effortlessly away from mine as if his presence would never be noticed if our eyes didn't meet. He seemed to shrink away from the afternoon sunlight.

Morrissey said, "Meet Pell Solder." Solder nodded without offering to shake hands. I figured, since Morrissey came to gamble, his pockets bulged with money, so Solder probably came to play bodyguard. If so, he didn't feel the job required him to talk. Four horsemen rode behind the carriage.

That was the end of the conversation. Morrissey occupied

himself with nipping at a silver flask and looking out the window. Cotton seemed as tense as a banjo string, holding tight to my bag on his lap.

I went to sleep somewhere along the way, awakening when the coach stopped. Morrissey grinned and tapped my knee. "Never saw a fighter who turned into such a bundle of nerves before a bout."

I stretched and yawned. "One of the joys of life, seeing new things."

He chuckled and tapped my knee again. "I like you better and better, lad."

A crowd formed around the carriage before I could open the door. A squat, burly redhead with a big towel draped across his broad shoulders smirked up at me and asked, "You bring a doctor with you?"

Innocently, I asked, "Is somebody hurt?"

The crowd roared with laughter, and he sneered, flexing heavy arms. "Not yet, but the fight starts in fifteen minutes. You better go inside and look at yourself in the mirror. You're not gonna look like that much longer."

Morrissey stepped out and said, "Now, now, boys. Let's not have our fun out in the street. You men go right along to the Spotted Dog and have a drink. We'll be along as soon as my fighter changes his clothes." He turned to the redhead and said, "Rube Cross, meet Rooster Delaney."

I stuck out my hand, and Delaney spat at it. He missed, so I dropped my hand and shrugged. Morrissey grabbed my sleeve and pulled me toward the saloon.

Rooster's cronies laughed when he shouted, "Your boy looks might pretty, Morrissey. He looks like a French dancer I know named Fifi. I thought you were bringing a fighter with you today."

Morrissey put on a politician's smile, shaking hands, waving, and patting men on the back. Cotton and I followed across the barroom, up the stairs, and to the door of a small chamber. Morrissey said, "Change clothes and get ready." He turned and stomped back down the stairs. The four horsemen who had followed the coach had mixed into the crowd and vanished.

I stripped and got into my fighting togs, tight pants and dancing shoes with the soles rubbed rough so they wouldn't slip. Some fighters wore a tight undershirt, but I never took to the idea. I felt they gave an opponent something to grab to jerk me off balance or hold me in a clinch.

Cotton shifted from one foot to the other. Mopping at his face with his handkerchief, he said irritably, "It's you who's about to have a fight. Why am I the one who's nervous?"

"You're not used to it. Just relax and watch my bag. Give me water if I ask for it. Hand it to me. Don't pour it on me." I rubbed cocoa butter on my face and upper body.

Cotton asked, "What's that stuff?"

"Slickum. If my man down there tries to grab me, he's after a greased pig."

I moved around the room, gently stretching and warming up until I broke a light sweat. After that I only moved enough to keep sweating and avoid stiffening up again.

Cotton walked to the window. "They're waiting down there. He's already in the ring. If you're ready, let's go."

"No, not yet. We'll make them come after us."

"What difference does it make?"

"We want to make him wait as long as we can. Gets on a man's nerves to wait in the ring. If he's an idiot, and lots of them are, he'll stand still, cool off, and stiffen up. He may even be dumb enough to take drinks from friends. Some fighters think whiskey gives them energy. Makes them drunk, that's what it does."

In front of a saucer-sized mirror nailed to the wall, I rubbed my hair and beard the wrong way. A man with his hair and beard trimmed and combed looks civilized. Fluff him up and he looks savage. I'd carefully trimmed both beard and hair to allow no opponent to get a grip.

I sidled up to the window and peeped out cautiously. A crowd of about two hundred men clustered around the ring set up in a field behind the saloon. Boos and catcalls signaled their impatience. Delaney slouched in one corner, legs crossed, leaning against the ropes. Someone handed him a bottle, and he upended it for three or four seconds. The crowd cheered him and then went back to booing and looking expectantly at the back door of the saloon.

The sound of footsteps clumping down the hall came again, and Morrissey shouted, "Where are you, me boy? Let's go."

I flipped a cloth jacket across my shoulders and nodded to Cotton. "I guess it's time."

When Rooster saw me, he waved me on with bottle still in hand, spilling whiskey on himself and three or four men nearby. Saloon girls wearing aprons with big pockets full of shot glasses moved among the crowd pouring drinks. The money went into the big pockets, but the men held on to the glasses. I surely hated to see a worrisome thing like that. I hoped those boys didn't get mad enough to start throwing those glasses. That can get to be a burden when they come at you in clumps of sixes and twelves.

Delaney came to the edge of the ring and stood in my way, glaring, making a big show of being ready to hit me if I tried to come through the ropes. I grinned at him, making no move until the referee pulled him away. Booing and whistling from the crowd made it nearly impossible to hear the referee, but it didn't matter. He just shouted something about the best man winning and motioned for us to shake hands.

Since Rooster seemed determined to try every dumb trick in the book, I figured he'd grab my hand and try a little knuckle crush. If that's what he had in mind, I tricked him and brought fire to his eye when I stuck out my hand but didn't shake, just slapped his hand away and sneered.

A roar went up from the spectators. Fight crowds love a grudge match. Rooster jumped forward, fists cocked, but the referee shoved him back toward his corner. I saw something I hadn't noticed before. The nails on both his thumbs had been sharpened to a point.

At the bell, Rooster charged across the ring. Dumb trick number one—try to rush across the ring and trap your opponent in his corner before he's ready.

Facing my corner, I pretended not to see him or to understand the screams of warning from ringsiders until he was almost on me. Then I ducked under his roundhouse swing, stepped aside, and let his own momentum drive him into my corner. Shoving a shoulder into his back to hold him against the ropes, I hooked him twice, left and right, gave him a wake-up shot to each kidney. Great eye-openers, kidney shots. Rooster rewarded me with a couple of explosive grunts of pain.

I backed away just in time. He spun around to face me with a wicked backhand swing. The clean miss caused him to flounder, off balance again and wide open. I snapped a hard left jab to the nose with all my weight behind it.

A jab to the nose can do wonderful things. It may bring blood and have a discouraging effect, and the bleeding may hinder the fighter's breathing. With a little luck, the nose will break. If that happens, the eyes often swell shut amazingly fast. Failing that, a hit to the nose always brings tears to the eyes, hindering the fighter's ability to see. All fighters use the left jab to sting opponents and put them off balance. Big fighters, if they work hard at it, can really hurt an opponent with the jab. I was a big fighter, and I worked at it.

Another nice thing about a jab, if one gets home, sometimes three or four more can fly in if they are thrown fast enough. Mine were fast enough. I landed four in a row, squarely on Rooster's nose, before he ducked to the side and shuffled out of my corner. The crowd loved it. For a couple of seconds,

Rooster's head rocked forward and back like his neck was broken.

When he shuffled aside and put a little distance between us, he arched his back and grimaced, still bothered by those kidney shots. I stood flat-footed, made a show of being relaxed, grinned at him, and jerked my fists up and down, mocking him for running away. Rooster showed his inexperience when he snarled and rushed me. Seasoned fighters simply ignore taunting words and gestures and get on with business as usual.

His angry charge told me he was a novice, and he paid for losing his composure by running squarely into two more left jabs. I leaned into them both, and he caught them coming forward. It must have felt like someone rammed him in the face with the end of a freshly sawed oak two-by-four.

The match had probably lasted fifteen seconds so far. Yet, twin streams already ran freely from Rooster's nose, and he was blowing specks of blood all over his chest and the front of his trousers.

He circled cautiously now, trying to keep his distance while he pondered what to do. He'd come in convinced he faced a pushover, and he hadn't figured out what had gone wrong. I didn't want him to have time to figure it out, so I feinted another jab. He ducked his head and tried to rush me. I caught him with two more jabs to my favorite red target and, before he could recover, threw my weight behind a right cross.

The lucky devil stumbled and caught the blow on the side of his head. Off balance but not hurt, he slipped and went down, ending the round. I managed to step on his hand and spin on it as I turned to go back to my corner. Screaming curses at me, he gripped the stomped hand with the other for a second and stared at it in disbelief. Then he sprang to his feet, and it took both of the men from his corner and the referee to hold him back until the second round started.

Rule one for good fighters—if you find you can hit an opponent with something, do it, and keep doing it. Stay with whatever works. Rule two—if you can hit an opponent in a particular spot, do it, and keep doing it. Even a light hitter can hurt you if you allow him to keep hitting you in the same place. Rule three—feel out your opponent in the first round. There should be no surprises after that.

Rooster didn't know how to fight backing up or circling; he loved to rush his opponent. When that didn't work, with me either stopping him cold on the end of my jab or circling to let him charge into thin air, he didn't have a clue what to do.

Built like an oak stump, he probably weighed more than I did and was bull strong, but he stood five or six inches shorter. His rushes to compensate for his shorter reach weren't working. He knew nothing of proper footwork—his predictable charges straight forward like a train on a track made him easy to avoid. His inept defense almost made me feel sorry for him. He knew nothing about fighting except to wade in swinging.

Rounds two, three, and four duplicated the first except for the knockdown. Delaney kept coming, but he never figured out how to avoid a stiff, straight left jab. With his nose jammed against the jab, his roundhouse haymakers couldn't reach me.

Rooster stuck with what must have worked for him before. He simply ducked his head and charged, and my jab methodically cut his face to pieces. Surely, he must have run straight into a hundred blows, almost all of them landing solidly.

I didn't try anything new, since what I was doing continued to work just fine. He must have tried to rush into a clinch fifty times, but I avoided him or shoved him away every time before he could get at my eyes with his sharpened nails. His groping hands couldn't find a grip on my slick skin.

Several times I'd simply put my open hand on his forehead to hold him away or to shove him off balance. He even tried to step on my feet to pin me down so he could move in close. Once in a while, I'd see an opening I couldn't resist, knock him down with a right cross or a left hook, end the round, and take a rest.

He got his arms around me once and set his feet, readying himself to try to crack my ribs with a crushing bear hug. It surprised him so completely when I sank my teeth into his neck he released me and dropped to his knees. Blood gushed from the bite, and I looked him right in the eye while I spat the taste of him on the ring floor.

Finally, in the eighth round, Rooster had cuts over both eyes, and they were puffed shut so badly I saw him knuckling his face, pulling aside the swollen flesh so he could see.

By this time, blood covered us both. The men in his corner kept splashing water on him, making the blood seem like ten times more than it was. Rooster surely had a broken nose, a painful but hardly a serious injury. Still, there seemed no point to punishing him further. He couldn't win. If he'd had a club, he couldn't see well enough to hit me with it.

Besides, the wind had gone out of his sails. Once in a while, just to add variety to what had become a monotonous bout, I'd hit him in the belly. The poor devil's stomach rebelled at the combination of whiskey and punishment, or maybe from swallowing his own blood from split lips and a leaking nose. I saw him dry-heaving in his corner after the sixth and seventh rounds. He had nothing left by the eighth.

Missing is the most tiresome thing that can happen to a boxer in the ring. It takes three times as much energy to recover balance after a missed blow than one that lands. My footwork so mystified him I'd hardly needed to block any of his swings. It was too easy to make him miss cleanly.

After the first few seconds of the eighth, he stopped charging forward and stood on unsteady legs, a hollow fighter. Still erect, he was finished but too strong-hearted to quit. Nothing remained of him but a helpless target.

I backed away from him, glanced at his corner, and gave a

palm-up plea. A slim man in a ruffled shirt, string tie, and gambler's black coat nodded and threw a towel into the ring.

When the referee raised my hand, the crowd turned friendly and gave me a round of applause. Relieved that the bout wasn't ending with a shower of shot glasses, I walked to Rooster's corner, ignored the hostile expressions of his friends, and said, "You've a great heart. There's no quit in you."

When he heard my voice, he spread the puffed flesh from one eye with his fingers and said genially, "You're too quick for me, Fifi, but you were slowing down. One more round and I'd have got you." His cocky grin, in spite of blood-streaked teeth and a grotesquely swollen upper lip, showed a spirit stronger than his brawny body.

Cotton followed me to the room above the bar and watched me sponge off Rooster's blood, dress, and carefully comb my hair and beard in front of the tiny mirror.

"Where'd you learn to fight like that, Rube?"

"I have two brothers."

"They must be terrors."

"Should you ever meet Ward or Milton Baynes, don't take them lightly." I smiled at his solemn expression and added, "I'm the gentle one in the family."

Morrissey tapped on the door and popped it open a crack. "Ready to go, lads?" I could barely make out Pell Solder in the shadows behind him.

We trooped down the stairs, waved to the men in the crowded bar, and climbed into Morrissey's carriage. The four horsemen seemed to appear from nowhere, slid into their saddles, and waited quietly, eyes scanning the street. As soon as the carriage lurched into motion, Morrissey ran a finger around his loosened collar and said, "First time I ever saw a fight won with just one hand, and I've seen aplenty. That's a wicked jab you have. I bet when Rooster shakes his head his nose rattles like a dice cup."

He pulled out a roll of bills, counted off five twenties, and stuffed them into my coat pocket. "You ever make any easier money than that?"

"Yeah, but not lately."

"Rube Cross. Where'd you come up with that name?"

"Cotton's taken to calling me Rube for some reason. I felt a little cross today. That's why I let that fight go eight."

"What was that? You *let* it go eight rounds?"

"I could have finished him in three or four, but I wanted a good workout."

Morrissey paused a moment, looking at me through narrowed eyes, and nodded slowly. "Either you're better than anybody thought or Rooster Delaney isn't the man we thought he is."

"You put me in with a couple of local chumps first to see what I can do. That was the deal. Rooster was the first chump."

"It's hard to whip even a chump without getting hit. Rooster ain't much for style, but I've seen him batter down men I thought were pretty good. In fact, I've won money betting on him. I'd like to see you tested a bit more before I put you in with the likes of Sailor O'Dell. I didn't see you get hit a single time."

I yawned and settled myself comfortably. "He hit me. Got me once with his third hand. I was pulling away, so he didn't get in a good lick, but it embarrassed me, that did."

Cotton asked, "Third hand?"

Morrissey turned to Cotton. "His head, lad. We call it our third hand. Boxers can ruin a man with a head butt."

"Win some money today?" I asked.

Morrissey's grin broadened and he said, "Did right fine, lad, right fine."

Just before I dropped off to sleep, Morrissey muttered, "Just a bundle of nerves, ain't he?"

I swear I think even greasy-eyed Pell Solder chuckled.

SIX

COTTON AND I stood in front of Chance Lorane's offices and watched Morrissey's carriage round a corner and roll out of sight. He asked, "You want to try to hail a cab, or you feel like walking?"

"Let's walk. We'll still be home by supper time. Hand over my bag. I'll carry it."

"Never mind. I don't mind toting your bag for you, Mister Rube. It's a lot lighter when the water jug's empty." Cotton took off at a brisk pace.

We walked a couple of blocks in silence before he asked, "Have you heard of Pell Solder, that fellow who rode with us and Morrissey to the fight and back?"

"No. What's worth hearing?"

"Solder's got connections with the Union Pacific Railroad board of directors. He does all kinds of contracting jobs for the UP. He charges ten times what the work should cost, splits the profits with the directors who help him get the contracts, and the stockholders get skinned."

"How do you know all this?"

"He's the only man I ever heard of that Chance Lorane won't oppose in court."

"Do you know why?"

"Yeah. Lorane told me the man's too dangerous. He said Solder's a cold-blooded killer. Anybody who gets in his way gets killed. You asked me about the way Lorane takes so many precautions, remember? I think it dates from the time he represented a group of stockholders out to get Solder. Three of those clients were assassinated, and the others dropped the suit. Lorane got shot at twice."

"Tough reputation for a man so timid he won't look people in the eye."

"Just a lesson for you, Rube. Things aren't always what they seem to be."

"Lesson accepted."

We fell silent until the Belle mansion stood only a block away. Cotton asked, "What are you going to say to Helen when you see her?"

"Hello, I guess."

"Is that all?"

"What're you getting at, Cotton?"

He gave me a sidelong glance and said, "She doesn't like you going off and fighting. I see you smirking, buffoon. No need to twist a crick in your neck trying to hide it."

"It pleases me to hear she takes an interest."

"Yeah, it worried me." When I gave him a questioning look, he chuckled and said, "No, I didn't worry about her taking an interest in you. I meant I worried that she hadn't taken an interest in men at all. She's twenty years old and good-looking. Lots of men have come around. She frosted their noses. I feared she might be a natural-born spinster."

I nodded solemnly. "They all fall for me."

"If you want to clown around, you can carry your own damn bag, joker."

"Now, now, don't get hot, Cotton. Fact is, I've got to where I can hardly wait till after meals every evening. The arguments we have in Mother Belle's downstairs study are the best part of the day for me."

"Arguments? Is that the way you see it? Not me. I learn more law during those discussions than I do all day long at the office. Helen reads for hours every day to get ready. She'd make a good lawyer if she were a man. Here, carry your own bag, I'm tired of it."

I took it from him. "I meant arguments like before the court, not arguments like getting mad and having a mouth fight."

Cotton burst out laughing and slapped me on the shoulder. "Mouth fight? That's rich. That's rich enough to be fattening. Sometimes you have a way of talking, Rube. You really do." He cackled like a cockfight the rest of the way home. Didn't seem all that funny to me.

Courtney opened the door before we could knock, looked me in the eye, and said, "Mother Belle would like to talk to you before dinner." Courtney's usually invisible Joseph made one of his sparse gestures at my bag. I handed it to him and tapped on the door to Mother Belle's study.

She glanced up from her sewing and nodded toward the rocker facing her. "You fought well this afternoon."

"Thank you, ma'am. News travels fast."

"I was there. I watched it."

"How'd you do that?"

"Joseph drove Helen and me to the fight in my buggy. Since ladies aren't allowed at ringside, we watched from the hotel next door to the saloon. We had no trouble getting there before you arrived and getting back before you returned."

"I didn't know ladies were interested in prize fights, Mother Belle."

She said softly, "I've been curious about you. Sometimes it's difficult to tell the difference between stupidity and ignorance. After watching your appearances in court, I've decided it's ignorance in your case."

"You were in the courtroom too?"

"Helen and I were there, yes. She said you wouldn't notice us in the crowd. She was correct. You spent all your time watching witnesses, the judge, and the jury. Helen said that would be your way."

"At least ignorance is something I can correct, ma'am. What can I do to improve your opinion of me?"

"I think you have to correct a severe case of arrogance. It's a common fever of the brain afflicting young males."

I straightened in the chair.

Seemingly satisfied with my new expression of serious attention, she continued. "I'm convinced arrogance, like a dark shade over the eyes, has caused your blindness. I couldn't comprehend it at first, but I can understand after seeing you in court. You really are exceedingly good."

After a brief pause, she continued. "However, as a person well qualified to judge such things, I can tell you that you aren't as good in court as you think. In the ring, you may be. Also, Joseph tells me your guns are in excellent condition, and they have seen much use. I suppose you're good with guns too?"

I forced myself to remain perfectly still. Instinct told me this old woman was about to tell me something important. One wrong word or unwise move from me, and she would stop speaking instantly. Cautiously, I said, "Ma'am, I was taught to try hard to do good work, that if I couldn't take pride in my work I needed to do it over until I could."

"Don't try your lawyer dodges on me. I asked a question. I expect a direct and truthful answer."

"I beg your pardon. I didn't mean to dodge. Yes, ma'am. I've handled guns since I was able to lift one. I may not be the best, but I'm better than most."

"Good. You work hard to excel at the things you consider important. Men who do that frequently ignore other matters, not recognizing that they can be significant too. Tell me, were you surprised to win any of your recent cases?"

"Yes, ma'am. Several times I just hoped to put up a good fight and cloud the issue. Ended up winning. Why?"

"Have you heard of Tammany Hall?"

"Yes, ma'am."

"Do you mean to sit there and act like you don't know the judges, the prosecutors, and probably the juries were paid?"

The silence when she stopped speaking settled over the room like a goosedown comforter. Once the suspicion took root, I could see dozens of hints that my plans in court always seemed to work too well, that I never seemed to face an unfriendly judge.

"You might have won a few of those cases in an honest court, but not all of them."

When I didn't answer, she said, "Maybe there's hope. I think I see a small crack in the armor of your conceit. If you're finally awakening, consider why all this is happening. You come, I'm told, from an outlaw family, yet you come recommended by a big southern law firm. Do you suppose Chance is building you a reputation for a purpose?"

I asked slowly, "What purpose?"

"Who knows? Chance Lorane learned his business from my husband. Believe me, Chance is far too smart to do anything illegal. But he does things every hour that you'd likely think unethical. He advises wealthy criminals, embezzlers, cheats, scoundrels. That's why he earns enormous fees. He'd never bribe anyone, never. But he wouldn't hesitate to suggest who might be bribed and how best to do it."

I stifled the answer which almost sprang from my lips. She already knew very well that lawyers seldom defend saints or angels. She would greet a response such as that with utter contempt. I asked, "Why are you telling me all of this?"

"Because I've come to be fond of Helen, and she's become fond of you." A trace of a smile cracked her taut face, and she said, "I might come to be fond of you too, if you ever mature into a real man."

Courtney tapped the door. "Dinner, Mother Belle?"

The ancient woman rose with obvious effort, smoothed her gown, and took my arm when I stepped quickly to her side.

"Coming, Courtney." She looked up at me. "You will be your charming best to Helen this evening. Is that understood?"

"Yes, ma'am."

She pulled me to a halt just short of the door. "One last hint, Mr. Baynes. Mr. John Morrissey is frequently the man who does the actual bribery for Mr. Tweed and others at Tammany Hall. Often forgiveness of gambling debts is a wonderful bribe, especially when rumor has it that men have vanished after they failed to pay debts they owe him. Has Mr. Morrissey offered to lay bets for you?"

I nodded, and she continued. "Think about it from Mr. Morrissey's point of view. Killing or maiming a man may provide a bit of gratification, even serve as a lesson for others, but it isn't a guaranteed way to get a debt paid. Forgiveness of a debt, a debt secretly paid by Tammany Hall, is surely more satisfying than violence which may or may not produce payment."

"Now that's a thing to know. Thank you, Mother Belle, but I have no idea how I might use what you've told me."

"Most men don't need to be in debt to be bribed. They simply need to be interested in an easy dollar or rapid advancement. You come from a family with an outlaw reputation. They'll hardly take you for a paragon of virtue. Today you proved you need money badly enough to risk your health in the ring. They have reason to think they can buy you cheap." Her piercing eyes held mine. "Are they wrong?"

"Yes, ma'am, dead wrong." I opened the door. "Hope I haven't made you late for dinner, ma'am."

SEVEN

THE DAPPLED GRAY cleared the fence easily, carrying my weight without distress. He picked up speed when I slapped my boot with my riding crop, easily avoiding the stragglers from the pack of baying hounds. We led the stream of horsemen behind us by an easy hundred feet, which put us in perfect position to see the end of the chase. The winded red fox vanished under a pile of snarling hounds, to be torn to shreds in seconds.

I wheeled the gray into a gentle turn and brought him to a comfortable walk away from the bloody end of a fine ride in the crisp morning air. Chance Lorane trotted his mount up beside me and blurted, "Damn you, Luke. I'd give an arm to ride like you." When I shrugged, he reined in to match my pace and said, "I'm always too far back. I always miss the best part."

My voice came out more sour than I intended. "Yeah, it was a great show. Twenty-five hounds on one tired fox."

"My, my. Sounds like you're in a great mood this morning."

"You know what, Chance? I've ridden to hounds eight or nine times, and the fox always got away. This is my first ride where they caught him."

"So?"

"I guess I'm a meat hunter. Killing something for fun didn't taste good."

He roared with laughter and slapped his knee. "There's a

couple of ladies' clubs who cry buckets of tears about us bad people who hurt cute little foxes. You sound just like them."

"I've hunted and killed many a critter. Can't say I didn't enjoy it, but there was always a point to it. It put food on the table or kept the stock safe. I don't remember killing anything just for fun."

"I see. You wanted the fox to get away again?"

"Yeah, I feel kind of silly, but I did."

"Well, most of the time you'll be happy. The little devils find a way to escape about nine times out of ten. Luke, there's a man I want to introduce when we get back to the lodge. He wants to talk to you in private. There's a little study at the back of the hall. I'll show you where it is. How about joining him there for coffee after breakfast?"

"Another rich man who wants me to marry his daughter?"

He stiffened in the saddle, then relaxed. Chance always took a couple of seconds before he could decide whether I spoke in jest. Straight-faced, he said, "Maybe so. Sounded like business. I didn't ask what it was about. Don't sign a contract without inspecting the goods. *Caveat emptor.*"

"Won't matter if the dowry's big enough. All women are the same except their faces. Their faces are different so we can tell them apart."

"Spoken like a dimwit bachelor without sisters. I worry about you, Luke."

We clattered into the cobblestone courtyard, surrendered reins to grooms, and went inside to a hot breakfast buffet attended by a swarming mob of servants. I finished faster than most everyone else as usual, excused myself, and sauntered over to a closed door Chance had pointed out. I knocked, heard no answer, and carried my coffee inside. The "little study" had three floor-to-ceiling bay windows and a conference table that would seat twelve. Books lined three walls.

I sat at the head of the table and enjoyed about five minutes of solitude before Chance came in accompanied by a strongly-built man with hair and beard lightly sprinkled with gray. Chance said, "Mr. Baxter Aldro, may I introduce Mr. Luke Baynes. Gentlemen, please excuse me." He turned and walked out, closing the door behind him. Aldro shook hands, went to the door, and stood waiting. At a light tap, he admitted John Morrissey, closed the door, twisted the lock, and gave a palm-up gesture, inviting me to resume my seat.

Morrissey gave me a big grin and a wave before he dropped into a chair. "Good day to you, Mr. Baynes."

I gave him a smile and a mocking little bow without rising. "Good day, sir."

Chance Lorane's abrupt departure and Morrissey's presence rang warning bells in my head. This had all the earmarks of a conversation Lorane wanted to be able to say he didn't hear.

Aldro spoke as if he were giving an order. "I presume, as a lawyer, you're a man of discretion, Mr. Baynes."

"You're free to presume whatever you like, sir. As a lawyer, I'm trained to avoid assumptions."

His eyes narrowed with obvious ill temper. Instantly, I took him to be an impatient boss constantly surrounded by hired men. His hands, as callused as mine, disqualified him from being a high-ranking military officer. He showed all the arrogant signs of a man accustomed to quick obedience, none of the indications that he had a sense of humor. My answer obviously didn't please him.

He cleared his throat irritably and tried again. "That was merely my way of telling you I'd like our conversation to be kept private, just between us."

"Are you engaging my services, Mr. Aldro? Otherwise, I caution you that the lawyer-client privilege doesn't apply. In the absence of that privilege, if you brag about how you robbed a bank, I'll call for a constable." I grinned at him. He had no way to know that one of my favorite games was rubbing the hair backward on grumps.

He stared at me for a long moment before he slowly lowered himself into a chair beside me. "I'm told you come from Louisiana."

I nodded. "It's nice to be told things. It's lonely when people won't talk to you."

He leaned forward and said harshly, "You seem to think this conversation is a joke, sir. I think I may be able to offer you a significant job, Mr. Baynes, but I need to find out a few things about you. I've heard about you. I'd like to verify what I've heard."

I shrugged. "I'm qualified to practice law, sir. Mr. Chance Lorane is the senior partner of the firm I serve. If you want references, you should consult him."

Morrissey laughed and said, "Maybe I can help, gentlemen. Mr. Aldro, I told you the lad's no fool. He doesn't know what you're about yet, so he's a bit cautious. Now, Luke, Mr. Aldro here raises beef in Texas. He and several of his associates are establishing branches of their business in Wyoming. There's an opening for a territorial judge out there, and the lads are looking for a man to recommend for the job."

I leaned forward to meet Aldro's hard gaze. "A Texan with influence in Washington? Now that's interesting."

Morrissey dropped his genial front and lowered his voice. "Of course, lad, it's a matter of money in the right places. You're a man full grown, so you know that nothing works so pleasant as when a bit of money smooths the way. It's better these days for a nomination such as this to come from New York than from Texas. Mr. Aldro here has the money, and I know the right people. This is a great chance for you."

Still meeting Aldro's stare, I asked, "And what's expected of me? Why would money be used to obtain a position for me?"

Aldro said, "We want a judge who's not a cattleman but who understands and sympathizes with a cattleman's problems. We're told you have relatives in the business."

I dropped my gaze to my hands, fingers laced together on

the table in front of me. Louis Flornoy had mailed my written personal history to New York ahead of me. Surely, Chance had read it thoroughly. Otherwise, I had mentioned little about myself to anyone but Cotton and Helen Sands. Mother Belle's voice came back to me, her comment that Chance knew who might be bribed and how.

I said slowly, "My brother's in the cattle business."

Aldro leaned forward. "Where?"

"In Texas, close to Victoria. Our family bought land from a man named Cowan."

"Well, I'll be damned! Morrissey, I think we've found our man." Aldro's surprise looked and sounded genuine, so I felt sure now that his information came from Chance Lorane. I had included only generalities about my family in the document that had been sent to him, but I had mentioned that Milt was a rancher.

Aldro turned to me. "That has to be old Caleb Cowan you're talking about. Your brother must be Milt Baynes."

When I nodded, Aldro relaxed and settled back in his chair. "I feel like a fool for not connecting the name. He ran a herd north this year. Never met him, but I've heard of him." For the first time, his expression thawed. "Caleb Cowan and Milt Baynes have the reputation of men not to be trifled with. I've heard that nobody in his right mind bothers their cows."

Then, as if ticking off points on a list, he continued, "You are a western man with no links to the Confederacy, a man fully qualified in the law, and a man friendly to cattlemen. Perfect."

Morrissey lifted a brow at me, and I said, "I'm comfortable with that description. One point I'm curious about, Mr. Aldro. When you say 'friendly to cattlemen,' what does that mean?"

Aldro leaned forward again, lowering his voice. "Since the railroad to the west coast has been completed, they're selling land along the right of way. Settlers are already heading out there like buzzards to a dead cow. That's bad enough, but there's even talk about opening the range in Wyoming Territory to homesteaders. If they do that, it'll be a disaster. Ragged farmers, deadbeats, thieves, bums, and every kind of trash will be dumped out there. That's just the sort of people who love to eat what they consider free beef. We need the kind of law that respects property, that doesn't burst into tears at every sniveling hard-luck story."

While I didn't agree with his description of the people who went west looking for opportunity, I didn't find fault with his basic idea. Few men would try to defend thieving.

I said, "I never held with stealing, if that's what you're talking about."

Aldro nodded and turned to Morrissey. "Proceed at once, Mr. Morrissey. How long before Mr. Baynes becomes Judge Baynes?"

Morrissey spread his hands on the table and smiled like a muscular, hard-faced angel. "Well, now, nothing's sure in love or politics, lad. But this is a case of either we can or we can't, and that's not a thing that takes a long time to find out." He winked at me and added, "Sometimes there's other bidders. We'll know in a week or two would be my guess."

Aldro said, "Mr. Morrissey tells me you are a promising pugilist, Mr. Baynes. I like that too. The rabble in the street can intimidate bookish men on occasion. I gather they'll have a harsh surprise with you."

Morrissey rose, shook hands, and invited us to have a drink with him. Aldro declined, and I mumbled about it being too early in the day. The door clicked shut behind Morrissey, and Aldro said quietly, "I wasn't exactly honest with you, Baynes."

I said, "Try again."

"I connected the name right off. I hoped to high heaven that you were Milt Baynes's brother. Wildest story I ever heard. Did you know Milt raised so much hell in Goliad they called in the Army to get things under control?"

"I visited. His wife told me most of it."

"Raising hell and putting a bad situation right is one thing, but he married old Caleb Cowan's niece. That's what impressed me. That wouldn't have happened unless Cowan judged him to be a true man. That old man would have killed him. Cowan's had the reputation in Texas for about a hundred years as a man who won't bend."

"You think I might be straight because you think well of my brother?"

"I got no choice. If you're a patch on your brother, you're tough, so crazy mean that nobody can scare you, and honest besides. I'm betting on it. If I lose, I lose everything."

I laughed. "You're saying you're bribing these crooks to buy a place on the bench for an honest judge?"

"That's the way the dishonest ones get in. Why not put honest ones in the same way?" Aldro rose abruptly, shook hands, and said, "I'll see you in Wyoming." He stalked out.

I tarried, looking out one of the large windows at the manicured gardens.

My path had taken a strange twist. I saw myself as a fairly clever lawyer, though still inexperienced, but now a complete stranger pulled strings and offered to pay money to put me on the bench. Rising fast in a profession by such unorthodox means carried little satisfaction. Aldro hadn't asked me to do anything I wouldn't do in good conscience anyway. Still, the arrangement had a bad odor. I found myself smiling at the vague reflection of the tall, broad figure in the glass.

Aldro figured he had me in his pocket, and he had all the earmarks of an implacable enemy if crossed. I purely didn't give a damn what he'd think or do when he found his pocket wouldn't hold me if I found it uncomfortable. Odd. He'd as much as said that was the kind of man he wanted.

EIGHT

COTTON AND HELEN followed me into Mother Belle's study and took their usual seats. Helen opened her leather-bound book and smiled at me. "I'll bet I've got you this time. I'm going to tie you in a knot before your dinner settles."

"I'll bet you don't," I answered. "I don't want to talk about law this evening. I received my appointment as a judge in Wyoming Territory this morning."

Cotton jumped to his feet and shook my hand. "Wonderful news, Rube. Congratulations. You're a cool one to keep it a secret all day, you and Chance both. I'd have been shouting it from the rooftops for hours. I thought I'd caught up with you when I passed my bar exams, but this puts you out front again. Will you make enough money to feed yourself?"

I gave him a weary look. His jokes about the amount I ate had worn thin weeks ago. "I'll be leaving tomorrow."

In the shocked silence that followed my announcement, I handed a package to Helen. She looked at me and held the gift as if she didn't know what to do, so I gave her one of my butter-melting grins. "Open it."

She made a big job of it, picking at the knots in the string until I stepped forward and cut it with my pocket knife. She unwrapped the paper covering and folded it like it was rare Chinese silk. Then she lifted the top of the box, sucked in a shocked breath, and closed it again. "Oh, Luke, you shouldn't have."

Cotton threw up his hands. "Oh, that's irritating. Shouldn't have what? What is it? Let me see."

Helen said sadly, "It's too much. I can't take a gift like this from you, Luke."

I said, "My mistake. Give it here, and I'll throw it in the fire." I reached for the box.

Her mouth dropped open for a second, eyes huge, but she recovered quickly and jerked the box away from me. "Don't you dare, Luke."

Cotton said, "Give me that," and grabbed at the gift while all her attention was on me.

"Quit that," she cried, pulled it away from him and backed away, holding her arms around it. "Stay away. Don't you touch it, Cotton Sands. I'll slap your sassy face."

"That's assault, isn't it, Luke? You heard her. A clear threat of violence directed at my person." He made a mean, snarling face. "I demand to know what's in that box."

She turned sad eyes toward me. "It's too expensive. I can't keep it."

"Scandalous!" Cotton barked. "Presumptuous, offensive, disgraceful. What is it?"

Helen stammered, "It's a . . . It's too much." She tried to peek again and watch Cotton at the same time.

"Luke, what's in that blasted secret package?"

"It's just a skimpy piece of hide from a Russian animal."

She pulled the top off the box and showed him the shining little fur. "It's a sable stole. Isn't it beautiful?"

Cotton put on a stern face. "I understand now. Helen, you're right. You can't keep such a gift."

She tried to look brave, succeeded in looking tragic, and nodded slowly. "I know."

"And you're right too, Luke. It should go in the fire since she doesn't want it."

"I didn't say I didn't want it." Helen sounded shaken. She touched the fur with a finger. "Anyone would love it."

"Seems to me, as head of the family, it's your decision, Cotton. Can your sister keep it?"

He shook his head. "Absolutely not. I fear if she accepted such a gift her virtue would be compromised forever."

Helen offered it back to me. I grabbed it, turned to the fireplace, and with the fur safely in my hand, threw the box into the fire. The flimsy inner wrapping paper flared.

"Oh." She squeezed her eyes shut and turned away.

I draped it over her shoulders. "Take a look in the mirror and decide if you want it."

Cotton said quietly, "Of course you'll keep it, Helen. Luke's a special friend. It's a beautiful, generous gift."

Helen preened herself in front of the mirror like an excited yellow canary, fluffing her bright hair this way and that. Then she darted back to me, gripped the lapels of my coat to pull my head down, and kissed me on the nose. She skipped to the door, did a comic little curtsy, and said, "Beg to be excused, kind sirs. I'm going to show Mother Belle."

Cotton dropped into a chair and raised a finger to his lips, signaling me to silence. "Let me just sit here a minute or two, Rube."

I stood quietly beside him and watched his chin drop to his chest, the smile still lighting his face, his eyes closed. After a moment or two, he looked up and said quietly, "We've been through hard times together, Helen and me. She's tough and smart and a wonderful sister, never complains. But I've never seen her so happy as just now. Joyful times should be savored. They're precious." His eyes widened when I slid the waxed wooden case onto his lap.

He slipped the two hooks on the near side and raised the hinged top. Inside were two matched, double-barreled, over and under derringers, with all the cleaning and loading tools snugly stored in cleverly carved recesses. Decorated in silver and gold, each weapon had a standing bear on one side and a springing catamount on the other. He turned to the gaslight and examined the spidery engraving on the brass plate centered in the top of the box:

ROLAND GEORGE SANDS
from LUKE SILVANA BAYNES, 1869

I said, "They're loaded, Cotton."

"Knowing you, I'd be astonished if it were otherwise."

He rose and placed the polished case on the table. Without a word, he put his arms around me and held tight. Slim and small-boned, Cotton seemed smaller than his lovely sister, almost delicate. Once again, he reminded me of Ward.

My youngest brother, the one so many people called a coldhearted killer, would come up at the most unexpected times and embrace me. He'd hold on for awhile, real tight, never saying a word. Then he'd turn his face away and walk off, leaving me blinking wet eyes every time. And that's what Cotton did. He gathered up the box containing his new derringers, ducked his head, and walked out. I knew I'd never get a more heartfelt thank you. Words sometimes simply aren't good enough.

I took a seat in front of the fireplace and watched the flames eat at a thick backlog. Cotton's remark stayed in my mind. Yes, joyful times should be savored. In a hard world, friends always provide the golden times in a man's life, friends and family. Cotton had become close as a brother in the months I'd lived in New York. In time of trouble, he'd be as welcome and trusted at my side as one of my kin.

My attitude about Helen troubled me. She'd learned every trick in the book about how to make a man feel chesty. Or maybe some women were born knowing. Every time I thought about her, memories of a thousand small kindnesses, graceful gestures, and ladylike courtesies sprang into the picture. She represented a contradiction I hadn't unraveled. While strikingly beautiful, the kind of woman who turned heads everywhere, she had a clear, sharp intellect.

I sat there grinning to myself, wondering where I got such a strong notion that beautiful women naturally came with empty heads.

Now, on the eve of my departure, I came to realize that I hated the idea of leaving, and I finally understood why. The more I thought about it, the more I felt dense, dull-witted. The only plausible reason I hadn't figured it out was that I'd been dodging the issue, simply not letting myself think about it.

I loved Helen. Obvious. Simple.

Scanning a distant slope when hunting in morning light, a man can look and look, then suddenly see a deer. The animal is there all the time, but the hunter can overlook it time and again. Maybe the deer needs to move, needs to take a step at just the right time. Or maybe a man's eye needs to be ready, needs to be particularly sharp, especially if he's not sure what to look for, or if he lacks experience. Helen had been there all the time, in good light, but I was just now seeing her.

Helen, Cotton, and I had spent most of the evenings discussing law cases since I'd been in New York. We'd worked out a wonderful game. One would be the judge, one the prosecutor or the plaintiff, and one the defense. Each evening, we'd switch jobs. Legal discussions invariably touched on ethics, values, attitudes about right and wrong. I felt I knew more about her than any other woman I'd ever met. I knew her so well her reactions had become predictable, and she strongly defended values I shared.

I sat up and chuckled, mightily pleased with myself. I had the answer. I'd dodged thinking clearly about Helen. I'd had a natural fear that she was so pretty that's all I'd see, blinded to all else. A man looking at a woman as shapely as Helen finds his mind occupied with all kinds of things that have nothing to do with clear thinking. I had a childish fear that a handsome face and figure concealed a cold heart and a mean disposition.

"What's so funny?" Helen stood in the doorway, smiling at me.

"Come in and sit down, Helen. I want to talk to you."

She sat next to me, holding her stole in her lap. "Cotton go upstairs already?"

"Yeah, and it's a good thing. I want to talk to you alone."

"Oh?"

"Yeah. How would you like to go to Wyoming?"

"I don't think I'd like it, Luke."

I couldn't have been more surprised if I'd walked into a door in the dark. We sat staring at each other for a long time. I guess both of us waited for the other to speak.

Finally, willing to lose the waiting contest, I said, "Actually, that wasn't the question I wanted to ask. I thought I'd kind of creep up on the real one."

"Luke, don't ask me."

That really stopped me. I couldn't think of a single thing to say.

She looked away and spoke sadly. "Luke, it's been obvious to everyone, so I guess you've seen it too. I've been attracted to you from the moment we met. The more I saw of you the stronger the attraction became."

Words that should have sounded wonderful turned ominous. Before she said anything more, I knew I'd blundered badly. This woman I thought I knew so well hadn't reacted predictably at all.

"All that changed a few weeks ago when I saw my first prizefight. I saw a new Luke Baynes, one I didn't know existed. Mother Belle explained everything to me while you were fighting. She was thrilled with you. I was horrified."

"Horrified?"

"Yes. Mother Belle said that man had no chance against you, simply none."

I spread my hands. "Boxing matches and horse races are never that predictable." She continued to stare at me, so I added, "But she's right. It was a mismatch. Something rare and unusual would have to happen for him to have a chance to beat me, but that's something nobody can really know ahead of time."

"Mother Belle said you toyed with him like a Spanish matador with a fine bull. She was absolutely delighted. She said you were a cold-blooded devil. She said you took him apart like a surgeon, dispassionately and efficiently. At first, I was so afraid for you I felt faint. My heart nearly burst. But then, I saw she was right."

"Maybe I can explain."

"Please don't. I know how persuasive you can be. This is hard for me, and you'll simply make it harder. Luke, seeing you in those circumstances made me fear you. I thought the fear would go away, but it hasn't. Well, it did for a few minutes this evening, but it's back again now."

"You're telling me I make you afraid?"

She nodded. Her clasped hands turned white with pressure, and I guessed she gripped them together to keep from trembling. "I see two men called Luke Baynes. One is the man I know with the gentle smile, polished manners, and a wonderful mind. The other is a beast, amazingly powerful and skillful, smashing another man without mercy, covered with his victim's blood, sneering, enjoying the pain he's inflicting."

I wondered if she'd understand the keys to my actions. An experienced fighter looks for clues as to whether or not a few simple rules will be enforced in the ring. And if the clues indicate a no-holds-barred fight, only a simple fool fails to react to reality. When a fighter knows that he's liable to lose an eye to a sharpened thumbnail, or maybe suffer even worse injury, he responds with his own defenses, stepping on a downed opponent's hand, biting in a clinch, butting, elbowing, throwing kidney punches, and on down the list. I decided she wouldn't be interested, only more deeply horrified.

She had said she didn't want me to explain, but she waited

while I thought about it. When I decided the explanation would only make me look worse, I said the only thing I could. "I can see why you stopped me, Helen. Certainly, I can understand how fear and affection don't mix. I never saw any hint that you felt that way. You cover your feelings very well."

"Oh, Luke . . ."

I raised a hand to stop her. "A smarter man would have noticed. I'm trying to get myself . . . uh . . . right side up again. You kind of tipped me over. You see, Helen, a few minutes ago, I thought I had figured everything out. I felt mighty good about myself. Things changed so quickly, and I was so wrong, I'm a little dizzy."

She came to her feet and handed me her stole. "I love your gift, Luke. I really do. It's magnificent, and it's perfect for me. But now you see why I can't keep it."

"Of course. A gift should bring pleasant memories. If it doesn't, it becomes a burden and an embarrassment."

"Luke, please." Her voice sounded like I was standing on her foot without noticing. A tear slipped down her cheek before she could duck her head.

She asked softly, "May I be excused?"

"Of course. You've been honest with me. That's always the best and kindest thing to do. Good-bye, Helen."

She flinched when I said good-bye instead of the usual good night, flashed a hurt look at me through brimming eyes, and ran to the door. I glanced down at the fur piece in my hand. A special gift selected carefully for a unique woman loses all value unless it goes to her. I thought about that for the longest time, stroking the soft beauty of the little garment.

My cup had been running over just a few minutes ago. Now, my cup felt drained, empty. Somehow, I seemed to have lost my lucky charm. I won a string of cases in court, only to learn that I couldn't have lost unless I shot the judges. I won a hundred dollars in a prizefight, money which came in handy, but I hadn't been in the ring since. An empty victory which started nothing and led nowhere didn't amount to much. I discovered I was in love only to learn that the target of my sentiment despised and feared me. I'd misread simple ladylike behavior, mistaking it for affection. Like a blind dog with a stuffy nose, I couldn't find a trail if I was standing on it.

My comment to Helen about things changing fast had been an excuse, and a poor one at that. Nothing had changed. I had simply been wrong again, confused, misled by wishful thinking. A man who's wrong about everything is always being surprised. So it turned out that big mean Luke was to stay the rootless member of the Baynes clan, the one still floating on the wind.

One last scan of the comfortable study brought a flood of memories suddenly turned painful. I was finished here. Wyoming people would regard me as a New York lawyer. So be it, but I'd never come back. New York gave me only empty victories and hurtful defeats.

Baxter Aldro had spread money around in the Machiavellian thicket of New York politicians, using John Morrissey as a guide. He'd paid to get me a position on the bench, so he'd figure he'd bought me too. When he found out otherwise, being a western man, a Texan, he'd feel cheated, probably pull a gun. When he did, I'd pull mine. Good. A man like me comes to prefer uncomplicated solutions. Most men who are often wrong like to keep things simple.

I pitched the sable toward the fire and turned away, closing the door softly behind me when I left the cozy study for the last time.

NINE

AT THE BREAKFAST TABLE, when I asked about Helen, Cotton said quietly, "She said she wasn't hungry this morning. I don't think she slept well, had shadows under her eyes."

"Well, I may be responsible."

He paused, fork in midair, and cocked a questioning eye at me.

"I got within an inch of asking her to marry me before she could stop me."

"Stop you? She stopped you?" He stared wide-eyed at me and lowered his fork.

"Dead in my tracks. I wasn't thinking, Cotton. I should have talked to you about it. That might have saved me from upsetting her. You could have steered me away."

Eyes narrowed, he touched his lips with his napkin. "I thought she was simply upset about you leaving. She looked like a ghost this morning. Tell me what happened."

"I finally figured it out last night that I'm in love with her. I asked her how she'd like to go to Wyoming. She said she wouldn't like it. Didn't have to think it over either, no head scratching or pondering, answered quick. Then she told me I was a beast and gave the stole back to me." I shrugged. "It didn't take long. It was a short conversation."

Cotton asked accusingly, "Called you a beast? You're setting me up for another outrageous joke, aren't you? All right, spring the trap. Let's hear the funny part."

"I take it she didn't tell you about it."

"You take it right."

"Well, I'm not proud of it, but I felt I should mention it to you. Like I said, I should have asked you about it first and saved myself an humbling experience."

"For heaven's sake, Luke, if you'd have asked me, I'd have said for you to go ahead and ask her. I thought she . . ." He rubbed a hand across his face. "As a matter of fact, I thought she . . . Well, never mind." He picked up his fork, put it back down, and came to his feet.

"What're you doing, Cotton?"

"This doesn't make sense. I'm going upstairs and find out what's going on."

"No, you're not. Sit."

Cotton dropped back into his chair, leaned forward, and stared at me.

"Stop and think about it. What's just about the most embarrassing thing you can think of to happen to a sensitive woman? How about some idiot offering to share his life, and her having to say no? Isn't that pleasant, to have to hurt somebody's feelings like that? She's upset. Leave her alone. She'll be fine when I'm gone. Coffee?" I offered the pot.

He nodded absently. "Luke, can you take a later train? I'd like to have a chance to talk to her before you leave."

"Pass your cup." He extended his cup, and I filled it. "No, I leave in less than an hour. Let her be. She's missing her breakfast to avoid me. Don't you understand that? But you don't need to go hungry. Eat."

Still sitting on the edge of his chair, he leaned forward a bit more and said in a low voice, "You know, uh, she's not experienced. Maybe you scared her. You didn't, uh . . . ?" His voice died away.

I gave him a straight look. "I didn't touch her, you cretin. What a dirty mind. You ought to be ashamed."

Blushing furiously as only pale-haired people can, he slapped the table, rattling plates and rocking cups. "What happened then? Something's wrong, terribly wrong. She's been driving me mad. It's been 'Do you think Luke will like this dress? What will Luke think about my hair?' It's been Luke this, Luke that, Luke some other thing every five minutes." He took a deep breath and came to his feet again.

Courtney opened the door a crack. "Anything wrong? Did somebody drop something?"

I shook my head. "No."

"Need anything?"

"No, thanks. Everything's fine."

She gave the tense Cotton, standing with fists clenched, a questioning glance before looking back at me. "Joseph has the horses hitched and your trunks loaded. He's ready to take you to the train station when you're finished with your breakfast. If you gentlemen are going to yell and fight, go out in the back yard. Don't break my dishes."

I folded my hands and bobbed my head like a Chinese coolie. She smiled and closed the door.

When I pointed at his chair, Cotton sat again. I dropped a hand on his shoulder and shook him gently. "Relax, friend. If you find I've behaved badly toward Helen, you can come straight to Cheyenne and shoot me. Write before you come. I'll send you train fare. There's no hurry. Eat your breakfast."

"You're covering up, aren't you, making jokes like this?"

"Yes, I'm trying hard to act like a big boy and a good sport. Eat."

Courtney popped the door open again. "I packed a basket with enough food to keep an infantry regiment for a week. It should last you till about noon. It's in the buggy. I couldn't figure out how to pack ten gallons of coffee and keep it hot. You'll have to find some along the way."

I dropped my hand from Cotton's shoulder to turn so I could give her a leer. "Poison Joseph and come with me. We'll live happily in sin forever. I'm a judge. I won't let the law get anywhere close to you."

She nodded instantly. "Good idea. I'll be ready in five minutes." The door swung shut.

Cotton began to relax. He gave me a disgusted look and said, "This is like trying to have a serious discussion with a man who's chatting with a broken cuckoo clock. I can't wait for that damned door to be jerked open again."

I pulled a paper from my coat pocket. "I almost forgot. This is for you."

He took it and studied it. When he looked up with wide eyes, I said, "I came to like that gray. You don't need to wear spurs with him. Just slap your boot with your crop, and he'll try to jump out from under you. He'll run his heart out."

"That's an expensive horse. You can't just give him to me. I'll sell him for you, Luke."

"Ride him for me, friend. He's yours. He'd never make it out west. He'd suffer. A good traveling horse out there needs to live on grass. He's been grain-fed and treated gently all his life. I want him to be looked after. You'll do that for me, won't you?"

"I could send him to you by rail. You'll be living in town yourself."

"Probably not for long. I think I'm a mover, Cotton." I took a deep breath and added, "I thought Milt would be the gypsy in the family, but a redhead captured him and tied him to a bedpost down in Texas. Looks like I'm the rolling stone."

I stepped to a chair in the corner and picked up a gun belt. He watched me without a word while I strapped it on and picked up the other. When I had the belts crossed and settled just right, I spun the cylinder on each of my Navy Colts, carefully checking the loads one more time before easing them into the holsters.

"You mind if I don't go with you? I hate good-byes."

"Me too. So long, Cotton."

"So long, Luke."

We shook hands, and I walked out the back door, giving Courtney a pat on the cheek when I passed through her kitchen. I'd already said my good-bye to Mother Belle, who rose with the chickens but never touched breakfast. She hadn't said much. Mother Belle tended to prefer being left alone most days till sometime after lunch. Joseph drove me through cold rain to the station, helped me check my luggage, and headed home with a cheerful wave.

Through a slowly moving rain-streaked window, I watched New York slide by, dirty snow crusted in dark corners. A conductor came past to check tickets, noticed my guns, and started to say something. He looked into my face, changed his mind, and went on down the aisle.

A man across from me asked, "Are you a lawman, sir?"

"No," I answered curtly, "I'm a lawyer. There's a hell of a difference."

Dropping my hat over my eyes to shut him up, I settled myself in preparation for a couple of days of butt-numbing pleasure on a swaying, drafty, grimy iron horse. Courtney's basket sat on the seat beside me. Several passengers walked past and paused briefly. When I looked up, they moved on. Nobody asked me to move it for the first two or three hours.

Then a pretty young woman stopped beside me. She'd been seated farther down the aisle, facing a leering drummer, and I suppose she got tired of it. I glanced up and down the car, saw no other empty seats, and moved the basket. She sat down, smiled like an innocent child, and asked, "Are you going far?"

I thought about that for a moment before I answered slowly, unable to make myself return her smile, "Yes, ma'am, as far as a beast can go and still stay on the high road."

Her eyelids fluttered a couple of times while she pondered that. She said, "That's nice," and didn't pester me again.

If somebody had to occupy the seat beside me, at least I had the good fortune she turned out not to be a chatterbox. The girl knew how to keep her mouth shut. After facing that stupid drummer, I guess she appreciated being left alone as much as I did.

TEN

I STEPPED DOWN from the train in Cheyenne feeling and smelling like a sour-mouthed grizzly, stiff in every joint from more than three days on a seat designed for an underfed Lilliputian.

I asked a man who sat on a flat-bed wagon in front of the station if he'd take me to my hotel. He looked at me, spat tobacco juice near my feet, and said, "Two dollars."

I claimed my trunks and helped him swing them aboard his wagon. The girl with the innocent smile stood between me and the meager lantern light from the station window. Her skirt billowed in the icy wind. The feeble background glow turned her small figure into a forlorn silhouette.

Four or five men lined the shadowy platform behind her, and I could hear laughter over the whining wind.

She looked up, startled, when I loomed over her. I asked gently, "Someone meeting you, ma'am?"

A hulking figure lurched out of the shadows. "Run along, dude. I'll look after her." He reached out to shove me aside. In that instant, the tiredness and depression dropped away from my shoulders, and I felt wonderful.

He never saw me draw. I stepped back, leaving him off balance when he shoved at thin air. Without cocking the Navy, I swung a right hook to the body with every ounce of my weight behind it. Aimed at him like the point of a knife, the muzzle drove into him with an ugly, sickening crunch. He doubled up with an explosive gasp of agony and dropped to the platform.

His friends surged forward together, but they stopped when I fired the Navy into the boards at their feet.

I raised my voice to be sure they heard me over the wind. "I'll count to three. Then I'll shoot at men, not boards."

If I had made the count, they wouldn't have heard it. They got themselves out of earshot with their first few steps into the wind.

I spun the cylinder so the hammer would rest on the fired cap and dropped the Navy back into its holster. The young woman hadn't moved an inch. "May I offer you a ride, ma'am?"

"Who are you, sir?"

"Beg your pardon, ma'am. I should have introduced myself on the train, but I didn't want to seem forward. I'm Judge Luke Baynes."

"I'm Nancy Aldro. My father was supposed to meet me at the station, but I guess he's been delayed. I'd better wait here. He wouldn't know where to find me if I left."

Her name hit me like a sneak punch, left me standing speechless. I hardly heard the rest of her remarks because I was so busy wondering if I had ridden all the way from New York with Aldro's daughter without knowing it.

My driver asked sharply, "Hey, mister, you coming or not?"

"Miss Aldro, do you live in town?"

"No, we live about a day's ride from here."

"You can't stand out here all alone in the dark street. This wind will make you sick. Why don't you come to the hotel with me. If your father doesn't show up, you can get a room."

"What about him?" She motioned to the downed man.

"You feel better yet, Sir Galahad?"

His voice came out low and thin. "I need a doctor. I'm hurt bad."

"All right, get up and get on the wagon. I'll try to find a doctor for you."

The wagon driver stepped down and spoke in a civil tone for the first time. "I know where a doctor lives. Miss, let me help you with your bag."

"Why, thank you," she said sweetly.

"Anything to keep from sitting here all night and freezing to death." He raised a finger toward me and said, "That'll be another two dollars," and cackled like he'd sprung the best joke of the day. He stowed her luggage on the wagon.

I said, "Get on the back with me, Sir Galahad. We'll let the lady ride on the seat."

He couldn't straighten all the way, shuffled hunched over with his hands pressed to his side. It took him two or three tries before he found a way to climb onto the wagon bed. He crouched on his knees and said with his slow, wheezing voice, "I can't sit down. The first bump we hit would kill me."

"Drive at a walk. Keep it slow," I said to the driver.

"Oh, I wouldn't want to get in no hurry. Wouldn't want to kill my horses in this heat. Another dollar for that fellow."

"All right. Get on with it."

The drive didn't take long, even at a walk. Nobody tried to talk in the icy wind. We stopped by the gate of a picket fence. I helped Sir Galahad down from the wagon and held his arm during the short walk to the house. The door opened quickly at my knock.

I said, "I found this on the street. It needs patching."

The red face with a gray handlebar mustache showed no expression. He said, "Come in." His gaze went over my shoulder and he added, "Go to the woodpile and get a couple of sticks for the stove, Jed. Come in and get warm, young lady."

Jed turned away, evidently heading for the woodpile. We stepped into the doctor's waiting room. He stuck out his hand and said, "I'm Doc Jordan. What happened?"

I shook hands. "Luke Baynes. This is Miss Nancy Aldro. I think this man walked into something in the dark, Doctor Jordan. We found him down by the train station."

After a quick nod to the girl, he looked at Sir Galahad. "Where does it hurt?"

"I think I've got broken ribs, Doc. I can't hardly breathe."

"If you'll take a seat and excuse us, Miss Aldro, I'll take a look at this man." He stepped into an adjoining room and lit a lamp. I followed, steadying Sir Galahad, who looked pale as death in the bright light. Jordan perched him on an examining table and helped him remove his coat and shirt.

"What happened to you, son? That's a deep, severe injury. Looks like somebody hit you with a hammer."

Galahad glanced at me, and said, "I ran into something."

"You must have been running mighty fast." Jordon followed time-hallowed medical practice. He poked repeatedly at the bruise.

His patient flinched and gasped, "Ow! Don't do that! For heaven's sake."

Finally, Jordan wrapped a long strip of heavy cloth tightly around Galahad several times and pinned it. "Son, you need to walk just a few steps through that door there. We'll pull off your pants and boots and put you to bed."

"You want me to stay here?"

"You have a nasty broken rib, splintered, in fact. I just hope a bone sliver didn't puncture a lung. I'm going to keep an eye on you for a day or so."

After we helped him into bed, the doctor looked at me and jerked his head toward the door. Galahad, through clenched teeth, said, "I want to talk to you before you leave, Judge Baynes." He cut his eyes toward Jordan.

After a surprised glance at me when he heard "judge" added to my name, Jordan said, "I'll wait in the other room."

As soon as the door shut behind the doctor, Galahad said, "I'm Jeremy Pitts. Are you a real judge? No joke?"

"I am."

"Judge Baynes, are you going to put the law on me?"

"Don't think so."

"Listen, I wanted to meet that girl, but I couldn't get up the nerve. Then I thought I'd act protective, run you off, and be a big hero. I didn't mean that girl no harm. If you spread it around this town that I acted improper toward a woman, they'll believe you, you being a judge and all. They'll tar and feather me. They might even lynch me." His head dropped back on the pillow, beads of sweat on his forehead.

"I never took to loose talk nor to lynchings."

"Thanks, Judge, you won't be sorry."

"I've got to get that girl to the hotel."

He nodded. "Judge?"

I stopped at the door and looked back over my shoulder.

"I got no money for a doctor."

I peeled off ten dollars and handed it to him. "If he needs more, he'll probably let you pay him later."

"Judge?"

I turned back from the door again.

"I got no hard feelings. Hope you feel the same."

"We're quits, Jeremy."

I went back to the waiting room. Doc Jordan, Jed, and Miss Aldro stood around the potbellied stove. Jordan asked bluntly, "How'd you do it?"

"Do what?"

"That's a terrible wound. How'd you do it?"

"I poked him with my revolver."

"Stabbed him, you mean. If he hadn't been wearing a thick coat, I'll bet that wound would be a penetration. I hope he doesn't have a punctured lung. If he does, it might kill him."

Jed spoke impatiently. "Can we go? I used to be married. I'd like to go home and see if she's still hanging around."

We trooped out into the cold. I rode in the back with the luggage again. Jed whipped the horses into a run, so we got to the hotel quickly. When we stopped, I jumped down with a fresh layer of dust over my expensive New York outfit. Jed took his five dollars, spat courteously downwind, and wheeled away.

I didn't even feel surprised when the hotel clerk said, "We just have one room, the one we reserved when we got your telegram, Judge."

I just took a deep breath. No help for it. "Good night, ma'am. Surely your family will come looking for you tomorrow." I turned to the clerk and asked, "Can I leave my stuff here till I can come back for it?"

He said, "Sure," and helped me tuck my trunks into a small room behind the hotel desk.

"Where will you go?" she asked. "I feel terrible about this. I hate to take your room away from you."

"I'll make do."

She had a point-blank way of looking at people that took some getting used to, a grown woman with the open gaze of a child. "You're like two men. You don't even look the same."

"Beg pardon, ma'am?"

"During all those days on the train you looked grim as a hangman. Hours passed and you never spoke a word. Now you look like a different person. You really needed to hit somebody, didn't you?"

This tiny filly made me feel uneasy and embarrassed, like she'd been sneaking peeks into my private diary. "You read sign mighty well, ma'am. Do you tell fortunes too?"

I glanced at the clerk. "Where's the closest hotel?"

"There's three others, but that won't help you, Judge. They're cheaper than us, and they always fill up first."

"Where's the marshal's office?"

"Town marshal or U.S.?"

"U.S."

"One block down and across the street."

I tipped my hat to Miss Aldro and walked out into the cold

again. By the time I knocked on the marshal's door, I was half frozen. I tried the knob and found the door locked. I took a couple of steps and looked through a frosted window while a lanky figure rose from behind a desk and strolled toward me. He peered through the window for a few seconds, watching me turn to a block of ice, before he opened the door a crack.

"Help you?"

I shoved the door open, knocking him back a couple of steps, and walked to the stove.

"Don't stand on ceremony. Just bust on in."

"I'm Luke Baynes, new territorial judge."

"Got your telegram that you were coming. I'm Marshal Ben Lorimer." He grimaced at my cold grip and rubbed his hand on his britches leg to warm it. "Great thing that telegraph."

"I'm told the hotels are full. You got an open bunk?"

He shook his head. "Got a couple of men on the floor already. You want to hold court now? Might make room."

"I'm too tired for that. Got any ideas?"

"I could lend you a couple of blankets. You could sleep on my desk."

"Keep it reserved for me. I'm going to look around."

I walked out into the cold again. Two blocks and two hotels later, I detoured into a saloon. A few words with the bartender and two flights of stairs later, I knocked on a door. I introduced myself and applied my enormous powers of persuasion, using my butter-melting smile and a peek at my bankroll. The combination worked.

Turned out to be costly, but it made a good story later. I spent my first night in Cheyenne in a perfumed feather bed. I had a bath and drank a pot of the best coffee I ever touched.

When I woke the next morning, I found my suit had been sponged and brushed. My shirt had been washed during the night and ironed dry. My boots shone with fresh polish.

LaRue Deveroux, owner of the bed and the saloon, who

wasn't half as tough as she looked and talked, made me promise I'd never admit I slept alone. She said it would cause loose talk and do grievous harm to both our reputations.

ELEVEN

BY TEN O'CLOCK the next morning, I had presided over my court for the first time and waded through a docket of minor offenses. All my criminals looked gravely hung over, and none of them wanted anything to do with lawyers or not-guilty pleas.

My first stop after leaving the courtroom cheered me. The general store had a sheepskin coat with unsheared wool turned inward that fit me to perfection. Slit up the back for comfortable use by a horseman, it reached to my knees. Even the sleeves were long enough. A wool scarf cut from a thick blanket and a pair of rabbit-skin gloves with the soft fur turned inside completed my purchases.

I dropped by the hotel at noon, figuring Nancy Aldro would be gone by then and I could claim my room. But when I asked, the clerk said, "She hasn't come downstairs yet."

"What's the number?"

"Room 203."

"Reserve another room for me, starting tonight. I'll pay by the week."

He spun the register for me to sign and handed me a key.

Her door opened quickly at my rap, and a happy smile died when she drew back. "Oh, you startled me. I thought my father had found me at last."

"Is your father Baxter Aldro, ma'am?"

"Yes. Do you know my daddy?"

"I met him once. Why don't you let me rent a buggy and take you home?"

She gave me a timid grin. "I'm afraid I'm caught in embarrassing circumstances."

"Would you care to join me for lunch? If there's a problem, we'll just talk it over and find a solution."

She didn't hesitate. "Thank you. I will."

As soon as we were seated in the hotel dining room, she said bluntly, "I spent almost all the money I had for the train ticket. If you hadn't shared your basket of food, I'd have gone hungry on the train. I can't even pay for my room."

"Don't worry about that. I'll take care of it. I'm happy to be of assistance."

"Thank you, Judge Baynes, but don't worry. My father will compensate you."

"That won't be necessary."

She gave a delighted laugh and said, "That's wonderful, but he'll still insist."

"Do you suppose your father didn't receive your wire that you were coming, Miss Aldro?"

"Oh, no. Daddy answered it. He forbade me to come to Wyoming. He says the place they have up here is still too rough and uncomfortable. He told me to stay at the school in New York. I graduated, but they wanted to hire me to stay and teach. My father wants me to do it for a year, but I won't."

"You sound like you didn't like school much."

"I loved school, but all the students and teachers were women. I grew up with men around me. I like men." Her eyes met mine squarely, as usual, and showed no trace of humor. She wasn't playing the coquette, just candidly stating an opinion.

"Have you ever been out here before?"

"No. I went to New York from Texas. This is my first trip to Wyoming."

"Well, let's eat. I'll hire a rig and take you home tomorrow."

After lunch, I escorted her back upstairs. Then I carted my belongings from the storage chamber behind the hotel desk to my room two doors down the hall from hers.

Luckily, it was Friday. I dropped by to tell the marshal that court wouldn't open Saturday. When I told him I was taking Miss Aldro home, he gave me directions. He said the Aldro place was a day's ride from Cheyenne. That meant I could get her home and come back in time to hold court on Monday. Standing with his back to the glowing stove, he ended with a grin. "You're in for a cold ride."

On the way back to the hotel I stopped at the livery, hoping to hire a covered buggy, but the best I could get was a flat-bed wagon. I rented it with a two-horse team for the weekend. Then I stopped in at the general store again to buy an ax, a shovel, eight blankets, a coffeepot, a skillet, food for about four days, a couple of tarps, a coil of rope, and a few other odds and ends. The clerk promised to have all my purchases ready for me to pick up in the morning.

No man takes to the road in cold country without a few basic items, and I didn't want to come up short on this little trip. Delivering his daughter half dead to a man like Aldro didn't strike me as a clever idea. Besides, since I was taking a wagon anyway, carrying a few extra things would be no trouble.

While I was at it, I bought myself a new Spencer. I went back by the livery, rented a horse, and rode out of town. By the time I came back, my new Spencer and I were friends.

Nancy Aldro had dinner with me that evening and breakfast the next morning. I picked up the bundle of sandwiches I'd asked the cook to prepare, told the room clerk to add Miss Aldro's bill to mine, and went to the stable to get the wagon. When I pulled up in front of the hotel and looked at the stylishly dressed young woman already shivering in the early morning wind, I just naturally drove her straight to the general store.

I bought her a sheepskin coat like mine, except it had probably been cut for a child. That coat, along with a scarf, a heavy wool knitted cap, and a pair of thick wool mittens, changed her fashionable big city appearance to frontier shapeless frumpy, but I figured she'd not freeze while in my care. The store clerk eyed me and said, "There's a dark line moving in from the north. Looks like we have some weather coming."

"I need to get the young lady home to her folks. You think we'll have trouble?"

"Hard to tell. When it starts to blow in this country, it gets almighty cold. You might want to take some firewood. It's hard to find wood on this prairie."

"Load me enough for an overnight stop just in case."

As soon as the clerk loaded the wagon we struck out and made good time until about nine o'clock. I broke the silence. "In this chilly weather, it's a good idea to nibble on something fairly often, ma'am. I brought food."

Her voice quivered. "I've never been this cold before in my life. I don't want to be a burden to you, Judge Baynes, but I'm about to shake to pieces." She must have been troubled to the point of agony but too timid to say anything. I needed to be more thoughtful.

I stopped the wagon and helped her down. I shook out one of my blankets and folded it into a pad to cover the board seat. Another blanket went across the back of the seat and down to cover the footboard. She stepped forward at my inviting gesture, and I helped her up. As soon as she was seated with her feet on the second blanket, I folded it up so it fell across her lap. I doubled a third blanket, got her to lean forward, and wrapped it around her.

"If you still feel uncomfortable, tell me. I'll put you back in the wagon bed. You can wrap up in blankets and lie down out of the wind."

She looked directly at me for a long moment as if she'd never seen me before. "You just don't have need of talk at all, do you? You haven't said a word for two hours. I was so sure you were mad at me, I was afraid to say anything to you."

I walked around the horses and climbed up on the seat beside her. I slid my blade from my boot, cut a sandwich in half, and handed her portion to her. As soon as we were rolling again, I said, "I beg your pardon, Miss Aldro. I didn't mean to be rude. I just didn't have anything to say."

"You're a peculiar man. On the train, you acted almost like you were mute. Even when you offered me some of your food, you used gestures, not words. I've never been around a person like you. You took up for me, a complete stranger, acting like the soul of kindness. But you struck down that poor man as unfeelingly as swatting a fly. You bought me food, lodging, and clothing, and now you're riding through freezing weather for a couple of days to escort me home. Why?"

I grinned at her. "You must be getting warm again."

"How can you tell?"

"Your voice doesn't shake like it did a few minutes ago."

She giggled. "When I force you to talk by asking a direct question, try to find out something about you, you change the subject. You're quite sly, aren't you? But you shan't divert me. Why have you done all this for me?"

"Maybe I took a fancy to you."

"Judge Baynes, I'm a very young girl, but one thing comes naturally to almost all women. We feel indifference from a man instantly. It's really quite chilling, even when a man covers it with great courtesy the way you do."

"Indifference sounds kind of coldhearted and mean. Most women seem happier if I keep my distance, and I like to see people cheerful."

"Gentleness comes as naturally to you as violence, doesn't it?"

We rode for quite a time while I thought about that. Finally, I said, "No, ma'am. I don't think it does."

She turned to look directly at me. That was her way, and I was getting used to it. I couldn't help but smile.

"What's funny? Why're you grinning?"

"I can't help myself. The thought came to me that you look like an owl. You always look directly at people, don't you. No sidelong glances."

She laughed, a comfortable cheery sound in the drone of the wind. "And you look like a bear. I wonder what's under that thick beard. I wonder why you think so little of yourself, don't give yourself any credit."

"I give myself credit, ma'am. For example, I've got good eyes. There are two men riding toward us over yonder to the left. They were going along their own way until they saw us. As soon as they saw us, they turned this way and pulled rifles."

My blade slid into the right pocket on my new coat and ripped through it easily. She watched me replace the blade in my boot and run my hand through the destroyed pocket. I shifted my weight so I could pull a Navy from its holster and lay it across my lap under the sheepskin coat. Then she surprised me.

"If you'll ease your second Navy to me carefully, they won't see from as faraway as they are. I'll hold it under my blanket. I promise you I can shoot it very nicely. My daddy is a good teacher."

The lady meant business, so I slid my second Navy to her and reached back for my new Spencer, covering the rifle from the oncoming riders' sight with my body.

With a round in the chamber and the weapon cocked and ready, I eased it into position beside my leg. With the Spencer wedged between my hip and the side of the board seat, muzzle firmly braced against the footboard, I wasn't worried about losing control of it. I never found the idea of shooting myself through the foot amusing. The sound of her cocking my Navy came clearly from under her blanket.

"Maybe there's no cause for alarm, ma'am, but since the war there's no telling what a person might run into. The way those boys pulled rifles right away didn't look friendly."

Her eyes fixed on the approaching riders, she answered shortly, "I saw that too. One of those horses looks familiar."

The two riders angled their mounts so as to cut us off, reining in directly in front of us. Each of them led two other horses, and the following animals bunched behind them. I pulled our team to a stop, holding the reins in my left hand. My right hand held the Navy under the flap of my coat, but I figured they'd think I was just warming that hand in my pocket.

When the wagon came to a stop they separated, walking their horses apart to approach us on both sides.

I said, "That's far enough, boys. Stop right there."

They reined in. One of them, the one on Nancy's side, said, "You're on private property. Turn around and go back where you came from."

Before I could open my mouth, Nancy said flatly, "If anybody owns this land, it's my daddy. I'm Nancy Aldro. Who are you?"

His eyes jerked wide in surprise, and he chortled, "Well, looky here. We got us a bonus, Lem. We already run off your daddy, Missy. He's long gone."

"You're a damned liar."

"Hoo-wee, just listen to that. It's gonna be fun to keep you for awhile and teach you manners."

His rifle jerked toward me, the snap of the hammer coming on cock sounding clearly. Nancy shot him a split second before he fired. Her bullet knocked him back in the saddle. His lead whispered by my right ear like the beat of a bird's wing. My shot, coming an instant behind hers, drove him straight backward over the rump of his horse to the ground.

The second man had a world of trouble, with too many things happening at the same time. His horse reared as he tried to bring his rifle to bear, our team bolted, and the horses he was leading jerked heavily on the lead rope as they shied away. Maybe seeing his partner go down shook his nerve too. Anyway, his shot went wild.

Our wagon passed almost under the belly of his pitching horse, so close I threw up my arm to protect my head from pawing hooves. I fired up into the rider as we pulled past him. We were so near I heard his grunt when the bullet caught him and saw his grimace of fear and pain as he reeled in the saddle and dropped his rifle.

Our team swerved and nearly upset the wagon while I fought to hold the reins and turn to see what was happening behind us at the same time. The second rider slowly slid from the saddle. I felt a tug and heard Nancy shout, "Turn loose!" She jerked the reins away from me and leaned back to put pressure on the startled team. In no time at all she had the horses back under control, swerving them in a wide loop through the tall grass, headed back toward the two downed men.

Both of their horses trotted a little way and stopped, looking back with ears pricked, led horses clustered around them again.

Without looking at me she snapped, "Watch out, Luke. Don't get yourself shot by a dead man." The words came out clearly, but her voice had gone strained and breathless. She hauled on the reins, bringing the team to a skittish halt.

I watched both men for a slow count of a hundred. Both lay on their backs, staring at the sky. Nancy had sense enough to sit still as a stone, didn't pester me with nervous chitchat. Without looking her way, I asked, "Can you watch that one over yonder while I look at this one?"

"Yes. Please hurry."

I holstered the Navy, lifted the Spencer, and dropped to the ground. "What's the rush?"

"I don't care about those men, Luke. I've got to get home. Did you see that roan mare the man I shot was leading?"

"Yeah."

Her voice came out in breathless hurried spurts. "That horse belongs to my daddy. Daddy loves that horse. He'd never sell her. The minute I saw her up close I knew something had to be terribly wrong. At first, I couldn't believe it. By the time I was sure, it was too late to warn you."

Both men were dead. As soon as I straightened after looking at the second man, she said sharply, "Come on. We've got to go see about my daddy." She gave a wavering little whistle and shouted, "Come here, Bets."

The roan trotted to her like a big puppy, pulling the other two horses with her. Nancy snapped, "Hold this team."

When I took the reins, she jumped from the wagon seat, tied the other two horses to the wagon, and sprang onto the roan, skirts going every which way. She galloped to the second rider's horse, grabbed its reins and returned. A couple of twists of her quick little hands and she had the horses tied to the back of the wagon. We'd picked up six horses in about as many minutes.

She sprang to the seat beside me and ordered, "Go. Go!"

When I had the team moving at a trot she tapped my wrist with the butt of my Navy. When I took it, she snatched the reins from my hands again and said, "Reload that and give it back." She whipped the horses to a gallop.

Reloading on the seat of a wagon at a thundering gallop isn't the easiest thing in the world, harder than on horseback. But I got it done, first the one she'd borrowed and then the other. All the time managing the plunging team, she got her flying skirts primly tucked, her blankets gathered around her, and her glove and mitten back on her right hand. No kitten ever squirmed around more gracefully, teeth and paws getting everything in order.

I said, "You're a wonder."

"What did you say?"

"I said that you're a wonder."

"What's that mean?"

"It means you've got pretty legs."

"Don't be crude."

"No, ma'am. I wouldn't think of it, not for one minute. That's the main thing I've learned today."

She was shaking like a snakebit colt and trying to hide the tears streaming down her chalky face. "Learned? What've you learned?"

"Not to be crude to a Texas lady. Certainly not if she's got one hand under a blanket." I handed my reloaded Navy back to her and watched her tuck it away beneath her blankets.

She broke at last. Between racking sobs she said, "I never shot anybody before. I think I'm going to be sick."

I took the reins from her and lied like a prophet of the devil. "You just creased him. No offense, ma'am, but it's a good thing I shot him too. I'm taking nothing from you. You had to shoot quick and you had a strange pistol. Besides, if you hadn't distracted him and shook him up, he'd probably have killed me." I shook my head and put on my saddest expression. "But don't try to cut a notch in that borrowed pistol. It didn't do the job."

She closed her eyes and took a deep breath. In a voice I could barely hear, she asked, "You're not just saying that, are you? Is that the truth?"

Stern-faced, I spoke with all the sincerity a good liar can muster. "I'm from Louisiana, ma'am. Maybe it's the French influence on our culture. No man from Louisiana would lie to a woman while she's warming a pistol between her legs."

TWELVE

HER SCARF SLIPPED, and before she pulled it back in place I saw her grin. I think she covered a blush at the same time, but it could have been high color from the cold wind. My mama taught me better ways to talk to ladies, but I felt the circumstances called for an exception. She needed something to get her mind off shooting a man and her terror about her father's welfare. Her streaming eyes and rigid face showed she needed distraction quickly.

Her voice came out muffled, but I caught an edge of wry amusement. Something in her tone told me she knew exactly what I was trying to do and went along with it. "Judge Baynes, you do have a direct way with words. I think I should be offended."

"I'm losing ground. A minute ago I was Luke."

"I like Luke. The name fits you, and it slipped out. May I call you by your first name? Do you mind?"

"Seems a bit direct to me, Nancy."

She chuckled. "My goodness, I'm finding a rough sense of humor behind that stern face. I'm going to call you Luke whether you like it or not. After all, you've practically adopted me."

"You willing to take a suggestion, ma'am?"

"Of course."

"You handle a team mighty well, but you better slow those horses. We won't get to your daddy's place very fast if you wear out those animals. I can pull this wagon, but I'm slow at it, and it nettles me to do mule work."

She eased back on the reins, bringing the team to a steady trot. "I'm worried about my daddy." She wiped at her watery eyes. "That's my daddy's saddle on Bets."

I took a deep breath. This put a new and more worrisome light on everything. It also answered the question that had crept into my mind. Even though her quickness kept me from being gunshot, she'd shown mighty little hesitation to pull a trigger. In fact, she'd been both quick and accurate, and I found that troubling.

His leading the wrong horse would make anybody suspicious, I had to concede that. I also had to admit she'd waited until she saw her daddy's saddle and heard the rider say the wrong thing before she cut loose. Even so, a woman so quick to burn gunpowder left me feeling a little uncomfortable.

She'd waited until he came up into sure pistol range too. That poor devil had been looking straight into two of the most guileless eyes in the world when he heard the thunder of his judgment day. If many Texas maidens were like Nancy Aldro, Texas gents probably got nervous ulcers trying to plan a simple courtship.

She asked, "What's so funny?"

I wiped off my sour grin and dodged the question. "All right, ma'am, we'll set a fast pace, but remember we have a long way to go. Marshal Lorimer told me we'd be near nightfall getting there."

The sun vanished behind racing clouds, and the wind added stinging sleet to its rising force. As fate would have it, we had to travel straight into the blast. By noon, I knew we were getting into trouble. As heavily dressed as I was, I lost feeling in both feet, and my hands ached inside my new gloves. I took the reins from her and stopped the team. "Get down."

"What?"

"Get down and walk beside the wagon. As soon as you feel warm again, jump in the back and get under blankets."

She dismounted so awkwardly she fell. I snapped the reins

to start the team forward at a walk and didn't look back at first, pretending I didn't notice she was down. When I finally took a quick glance back at her, she was on her feet and walking, obviously stiff and having a hard go of it.

I kept the team at an even pace. She fell behind at first, but her hobbling walk smoothed out after a few minutes, and she began to trot. Every time she slowed to a walk she'd fall behind again and have to go back to a trot to catch up. I waited for her to whine or complain. No such thing. She was shaping up to be no trouble at all. In fact, she showed every sign that she'd make a handy trail partner.

After about ten minutes of it, I asked, "Warm yet?"

"Better."

I pulled to a stop. She jumped onto the back of the wagon and crawled forward until she sat right behind me. I felt her head lean against the small of my back. Clever little baggage, she was using my bulk to break the wind. She let a few minutes pass before she shouted over the storm. "Luke, it's nice back here. It makes a big difference just to be able to turn away from the wind. I'm much better now. How do you stand it up there?"

"I'm a big strong man, and you're a sissy. I'm going to try to pass the reins back to you. I think they're long enough."

She lifted a mittened hand and took them.

"Don't even turn around, Nancy. There's no need for you to face that awful wind. I'm going to walk to warm up too. You just hang on to those reins and keep the team from turning away from the wind. Can you do that?"

"Certainly. Go ahead."

I didn't stop the team, just stepped off to the ground. The shock when I hit felt more like I'd jumped from a barn roof. My cold legs didn't respond, and I pitched forward on my face. The wagon rumbled past before I could scramble back to my feet. From the wad of blankets propped against the front of the wagon came a derisive laugh followed by a muffled "Now who's a sissy?"

My cheeks felt stiff enough I feared they might crack when I grinned. The first few steps erased the grin though, and I staggered worse than she had. The muscles in my legs had gone numb and my feet felt like wooden blocks, so I wobbled like a windblown scarecrow. It must have taken five minutes of struggle before my joints stopped creaking and my legs stopped feeling like they'd gone to sleep. By the time circulation came back and I could walk a straight line, I had to trot to catch up. I turned my back and trotted backward for awhile, trying to protect my windblasted eyes.

Again, the wad of blankets shouted over the wind, "Cheat. That's cheating."

"You're just mad 'cause you didn't think of it."

"I thought of it, but with the shoes I'm wearing, I'd just fall on my backside. You'd have another chance to laugh at me."

"I didn't laugh at you."

"Did too. You didn't look back because you didn't want me to see."

"I did not laugh at you."

"Did too." Her laugh came faintly over the wailing wind.

A peculiar glowing dusk had fallen at high noon, and I could only see about twenty feet through the stinging, swirling ice-filled air. Mixed snow and sleet drove endlessly past, seeming never to fall to the ground. Yet fall it did. The earth turned into a murky sliding carpet, tall grass bending low over the slithering powdery ice shroud. The mixture of sleet and snow fled from the wind in flowing streams and fans like ghostly sprays of frosted smoke. Weak light seemed to come as much from below as above.

"Luke! Luke, where are you?"

I spun around to trot forward again. The dim tracks of the wagon showed plainly underfoot, but all I could see ahead was a wall of white. Then a trick of the wind split the wall. Nancy had stopped. She stood in the wagon bed shielding her eyes with one hand, looking for me, blankets fluttering. I waved.

Her voice high and thin in the gale, she shouted, "Get on the wagon. I shut my eyes for a second, and you just vanished like some kind of magic. You scared me to death."

I ran past her and jerked the folded blanket off the wagon seat. After I flipped it a couple of times in the wind to rid it of its layer of white, I folded it again, slapped the slect off the seat, and swung up. She sat back down in the wagon bed like her legs had collapsed. I started the horses forward at a trot.

"Nancy?"

"Yes?"

"This is no good. We'll freeze to death driving straight into the wind like this. I swear, it freezes the water in my eyes before I can blink."

"I know, but we can't turn back. I've got to find out if my daddy is all right."

"We're riding right into the teeth of a storm."

"I don't care. I've got to go on."

After a few minutes, she yelled over the wind. "Luke?"

"Yeah?"

"You don't have to do this. Take one of the horses and go back to town. You'll be riding with the wind at your back. I can go on by myself."

"Nonsense. You're too little. You need a grown-up with you."

"What? I can't hear much through these blankets."

"Never mind. We'll make it."

She waited for a few minutes before she yelled at me again. "Luke?"

"Yeah?"

"Let this be a lesson to you."

"How's that?"

"You shouldn't pick up strange women on the street."

I mumbled, "Yeah, my daddy told me not to go to whore-houses either, but I slept mighty warm in one."

"What?"

I raised my voice. "I said I wish there were more houses along here. I'd like to warm up in one."

She climbed into the seat beside me and tucked another blanket around my feet. "Pull your knife."

Barely able to see her through my watery eyes, I pulled my blade from my boot before I even thought to ask why. That made me feel foolish when I blurted, "What for?"

"I'm going to flip a blanket over you. I'll tuck it in all around you. You cut a little slit to see through."

It worked. In fact, it made all the difference in the world. Busy little hands, deft and quick, shoved me this way and that, tucking the blanket under and around me to keep it from flapping in the gale. That blanket made a kind of tent to knock off the wind. I couldn't see much through the peephole I cut, but I couldn't see more than a few feet through the blowing snow anyway. I yelled, "Thanks, little mother."

A tiny fist hit me a pretty good lick on the shoulder. I felt the seat shift as she climbed back into the wagon bed. A moment later, she jerked the back of my blanket loose, put an arm around me to hand up a sandwich, and tucked the blanket back in place.

"Thanks, girl. You warm back there?"

"Actually, I'm comfortable. How many blankets did you bring, anyway?"

"Eight."

"Because you were escorting a sissy? Bless you, big tough man. Three for you and five for me. That works out just right. I love my new coat you bought. It's beautiful, and it's saving my life. You think of everything, don't you?"

"Yep."

About mid-afternoon we rode out of the snowstorm, but the wind never let up, and the clouds never broke. It took awhile before I noticed the difference, because the wind kept picking the powdery stuff off the ground and swirling it back into the air. The whole world seemed to be moving past, flowing by me like a battering cloud of white spray. It created the odd impression that the wagon had stopped, but the wheels still turned, and the shocks of passage over frozen ground still jarred my spine.

Though I was not an expert on Wyoming in the winter, it looked to me like more bad weather coming. The air had that sharp, brittle feel it gets when the temperature drops well below freezing. My bet was it must be close to zero and falling.

Nancy called out, "How much farther do you think?"

"We're coming to a creek right now. Marshal Lorimer said it was just a little way after we reach the creek. We'll turn and head upstream. It won't be long if the horses hold up."

Snow started falling again, and darkness closed in. My stomach tightened as the minutes passed without finding the place, but the snow parted again like a white curtain, and there it was.

I could see why Aldro tried to tell his daughter to stay in New York. He had dug into the south side of the creek bank and built what looked like two rooms and a stable. The low sod roof indicated a half-sod and half-dugout structure. Smoke coming from a tin stack made the place look mighty inviting to a man caught in a blizzard, but Aldro probably wanted more time to improve the dwelling for a daughter accustomed to something better. Still, he'd picked a good spot. Backed into the bank, the north wind couldn't attack the house, could only blast across the sod roof.

The wagon was only twenty yards or so from the house when I saw it. If the man Nancy shot had told the truth, if Aldro had been driven away, I was a cinch target from inside. Even worse, I'd put Nancy right in the line of fire too.

When all else fails, my pa used to say, bluff like the devil and grin like an angel. I turned the team toward the house and called out to her, "Look out, Nancy." Then I shouted, "Hello the house."

Since I had no choice, caught in the open and too close to try to turn away, I figured to ride up like I owned the place and hope for the best. It turned out my warning came too late or Nancy ignored it. She slipped off the back of the wagon, and I groaned at the sight of her walking straight at the cow-hide-covered door, a blanket around her shoulders flapping downwind like a broken wing. My only hope sprang from her flaring skirts and short stature. Even an outlaw might hesitate to shoot at that kind of target.

No hope for it. If outlaws had the house, they now had Nancy too. I dropped the reins, and the team eagerly headed for what I took to be the stable at the opposite end of the structure. I slid off the seat on the far side and walked beside the team, holding my Spencer in my left hand and the Navy in the right. At least, I hoped to present less than a full target. Nobody fired. I slipped into the stable, jumped away from the door and crouched low, Navy swinging from side to side. The stable was empty. No connecting door led to the other rooms.

I stood at the doorway, watching along the front wall of the building while the team and the led horses behind the wagon stamped impatiently, wanting to get into that stable as bad as I wanted to be in a warm house. Nancy had vanished inside.

Then she stepped out, cupped a hand over her eyes and stared at the wagon. I waved an arm to catch her attention, and she motioned for me to come in.

I shouted, "Come here."

She trotted to me. "It's all right, Luke. Nobody's here but my daddy and a hired hand. My daddy's hurt."

I pulled her blanket aside. Her hands were empty.

Always quick, she said, "I put your Navy down when I saw everything was all right. It's in the house. Come in, Luke. It's not a trick." She grabbed my arm and pulled me along.

THIRTEEN

SHE SHOVED THE DOOR OPEN and stepped in ahead of me. A wide-eyed youngster stood by a glowing potbellied stove, one hand hidden behind him. I leaned my Spencer against the wall and said slowly, "Don't show me a gun, young fellow. I'm nervous today."

Nancy shoved the door shut and snapped, "Bobby! Don't be a fool. I told you he's a friend." She darted to him and jerked the gun behind his leg away from him.

I unbuttoned my coat with my left hand and holstered my Navy.

Still holding his gun, Nancy said primly, "Judge Luke Baynes, this is Bobby Nels."

I stepped forward and extended a hand. He flinched like he expected a blow, then shook my hand with a hesitant grin. "I hope I never have trouble with the law. You look like the biggest, meanest judge in the world." He must have been every bit of fifteen years old.

"I hope you don't get in trouble too, Bobby. I *am* the biggest, meanest judge in the world. Where's your boss?"

Nancy answered for him. "He's in the next room." Her voice dropped to a whisper. "Luke, he's been shot three times." She handed Bobby's six-gun back to him, and he shoved it under his belt.

I pulled aside the blanket hung over the doorway and stepped into the bunk room. Baxter Aldro lay on a cot next to the back wall holding a six-gun across his chest. The man's face was pale as a china plate, his lips bloodless. His eyes followed me as I walked over to him, then shifted to Nancy when she stepped around me and bent to kiss his forehead.

"Can you talk, Aldro?"

"Why hell yes. I ain't dead."

"Where you hit?"

"Twice in the left arm, once in the left leg. They got the left side of me pretty good."

"Any bones broken?"

"Nope."

"Any lead still in you?"

"Nope."

"That doesn't sound so bad. Why're you lying around in bed before supper time? It's not Sunday."

His eyes drifted shut, but I got a shadow of a grin from him. He took a couple of deep breaths like he was taking a running start to get the words out and spoke without opening his eyes. "I bled like a stuck hog. I bet I haven't got a teacup left in me. I'm under four blankets, and I'm still cold."

Dark as a cave, the room held three more cots and a single crude table with a pitcher of water and a glass on it.

"Nancy, I'm going to unload the wagon and tend to the horses. By the way, you going to give my other Navy back to me?"

She stood beside her father, smoothing his tangled hair for so long I thought she hadn't heard my question. Finally, she turned to give me her straight look and asked, "Do I have to?"

Caught by surprise, I met her eyes for a moment, then unbuckled my second gun belt. "You might as well have the things to go with it so you can look fashionable."

She caught the belt and holster when I swung them to her. "Thank you, sir."

"You're welcome. I'll add it to my bill. You're going to have a hard time shortening that belt enough."

"I don't wear it around my waist the way you big fat men

do. I wear it over my shoulder." She slipped it on to show me. As a matter of fact, she looked at home with it, leaving no doubt that she was used to wearing one in that manner.

"That's fetching, ma'am. It'll start a fad. Every well-dressed woman will want one."

Bobby sprang from his seat on a box when I came back through the doorway.

"You work here, Bobby, or you just hold down that box?"

"I work here." He grabbed his coat from a peg and shrugged into it. "I heard you talking to Mr. Aldro. I'll help with the horses, Judge Baynes, but we gotta be careful. They been shooting at us." He pointed to the cluster of holes in the cowhide front door.

"They shot Mr. Aldro and my brother out on the range. My brother's still lying out there somewhere. Mr. Aldro said they just rode up and started shooting for no reason a'tall. They followed him home, shooting all the time, and run off all the horses. Me and Mr. Aldro shot back at 'em, but I don't think we hit nothing."

"How many?"

"Mr. Aldro says two. I only saw one."

"The war may be over. Two men tried to shoot me on the way here. They weren't up to it."

"You scare 'em off, Judge? You think they'll come back?"

"They won't come back."

He shook his head doubtfully. "I don't know, sir. They came back after we shot at them. I been afraid to step outside for two days."

"Bobby."

He looked up from pulling on a glove.

"You're a young fellow, and I know you mean no offense, but you'll learn more if you listen closer. I said they won't come back."

He looked up at me, his hands gone still. Slowly he said, "Yes, sir. I understand now. I didn't mean no disrespect."

"No offense taken. Now here's how we're going to work together. You dig that pistol out from behind your belt and put it in your coat pocket. If you need it, you'll need it fast. Next thing, you follow about ten steps behind me. If you see me look in one direction, you look the other. We cover each other. Understand?"

"Yes, sir."

"One last thing, take that lamp to Miss Nancy in the other room so she doesn't have to sit in the dark. Besides, we don't want light behind us when we step out that door, do we?"

"No, sir." He grabbed the lamp and walked to the blanket-shrouded doorway. His hand stopped about an inch from the blanket and jerked back without touching it. "Miss Nancy, can I come in?"

I turned away to hide my grin. The very nature of things changes when a lady is present, even in a crude sod hut with a dirt floor. Courtesy and respect beget quality in life, not bricks and mortar and fancy fixings.

We made it to the stable without any trouble. Darkness shrouded the prairie, but I didn't want to risk using a light. The two men I had left behind on the cold trail might not be all of the ones causing trouble.

By the time we finished it had grown so dark we had to feel our way back along the front wall. The air seemed almost solid with driven snow. Wyoming wind in the winter is the devil's knife, cutting deep with an edge so cold it burns.

Inside again, I peeled off my hat, coat, and gloves and spent a few minutes hovering over the stove.

"Nancy?"

"Yes?" She pulled the blanket door cover aside and gave me an inquiring look.

"I suggest we bring your daddy in here by the stove. He said he was cold. I figure to bring a cot in here for you too. Bobby and I will sleep in the bunk room. I'm going to tie that blanket back so a little more of the heat'll come to us too. You decide you want some privacy, just let the blanket down. All right?"

She nodded and stepped aside. Bobby and I picked up Aldro, cot and all, and carried him into the warmer room. Nancy threw together a meal, and Aldro surprised me by showing a good appetite. Nancy fed him deftly, as if she'd done it all her life. I wondered if the old man had been eating much since he'd been wounded. I couldn't imagine him accepting help from young Nels of the kind Nancy offered in the natural order of things.

After the meal, I asked, "You up to a little talk?"

Aldro nodded. Evidently he prospered under his daughter's care. His color looked better already. Peace of mind can mean a lot to a sick man, and some only thrive in the hands of kinfolk.

"What did the men who shot you look like?"

His description matched the two Nancy and I encountered on the trail. I told him about the incident and about bringing six horses back with us.

Aldro said that he'd never seen either of the men before. "I never thought anybody would try to kill two men just to steal a few horses. I was lucky. They shot Larry Nels, Bobby's big brother, point-blank, without any warning. I got away because I was a little distance off to the side when they cut loose. They chased me all the way back here. Bobby helped me run 'em off."

"You got any more hands?"

He shook his head. "Not up here. I hired the Nels brothers to winter up here and watch after things. I need to go back to Texas to get a herd ready for a spring drive."

"When did all this shooting happen?"

"Three days ago. It was the day before I planned to go to town to meet Nancy."

"Where did Larry fall?"

"You going after him?"

I nodded. "Seems like somebody ought to."

He told me how to get there. By the time he finished, his eyelids began to get too heavy for him, so I said good night and turned to Nancy. "I think somebody ought to stay awake tonight to keep the fire going. After losing so much blood, your daddy shouldn't get chilled. When you're ready for bed, call me."

She nodded.

I looked at Bobby Nels. "I'll take the midnight watch if you'll take the morning turn."

He said, "Yes, sir. That's fine with me."

I checked the bar across the front door before I went to the bunk room. Tired as I was, I hated to lie down. I'd been obliged to kill men before, and I dreaded the tortured nights that followed. Years ago, on the day my mother died, six stupid men came to our home to recruit me and my brothers into the Confederate Army at gunpoint. That day, my life changed for all eternity.

My family killed those men when they pulled guns on us. My pa killed one of them, the leader of the group, and he never looked back, nor did he shed a tear that I knew about.

My youngest brother killed three of the six. Ward came to be known as a fearsome, merciless gunfighter. He was nowhere near the cold-blooded killer people thought him to be, but I knew for an absolute fact that Ward never lost a moment's sleep after killing a man.

My next youngest brother killed one of the six. Milton, the family joker, our wild gypsy, never seemed disturbed by anything. Purely practical, Milt would be shocked at the idea of suffering over anything that was past. His attitude was that the past can't be changed, so only the future is worth thinking about.

I killed one of the six. Unlike my kin, demons came at me, found doubt and weakness, and pounced on me for months after that. Every time I went to sleep, they put terrible, haunting dreams in my head. Such terror and sadness racked me that an hour after waking I'd still be fighting to control the trembling. Finally they tired of the sport and left.

Then, two years later, I had to kill two Indians out of a bunch who tried to ambush us. My devils came rushing back. Again, the demons tortured me, jerked me awake time after time, sick and mournful, heart fluttering, pulse throbbing, muscles twitching. No matter whether I had any choice, no matter how righteous I felt about it, killing a man called down fiends on my head in the night.

The terror had already got me when Nancy put her hand on my wrist to wake me. Neither of us spoke. I rose and walked into the room where Aldro lay asleep. She slipped between the blankets on her cot and watched me shake.

I walked to my coat and pulled my Bible from the inside pocket. Nobody could read by the meager light from the stove vent, and I had no intention of lighting the coal oil lamp in the middle of the night.

I sat on Bobby's box near the stove, leaning forward with my elbows on my knees. I didn't want to read the Book. I just held it in both hands and rubbed its familiar sweat-stained cover against my forehead. It didn't help. Nothing did.

Maybe the Book was enough for some men, but paper pages couldn't comfort me, no matter how profound their wisdom. No matter. Sometimes a suffering man just has to have something to hold on to, and the Book was all I had.

Loneliness found cracks in my armor, let fiends get in to torture my troubled mind. Wind sang its cold song, sighing across the stark empty grassland, mournful reminder to a solitary man that he has no one to hold. I found one, the bright-haired Helen, but I lost her. Darkness is heavier after looking at the light.

Nancy Aldro never said a word, but I knew she stayed awake. She watched me for a long time. Without looking, I could feel her eyes on me. She'd pulled a trigger today too. But devils wouldn't come near her. They wouldn't dare.

When she spoke after such a long silence, I started like a spooked deer, nearly dropped the Book.

"My daddy says truly intelligent men always suffer from self-doubt."

I turned to look at her, but she rolled in her blankets to face the wall. She'd said all she intended.

FOURTEEN

THE WIND blew itself out early in the morning. After the continuous din, the quiet seemed ominous. I shrugged into my coat. Since the sod hut had no windows, I opened the door cautiously and stepped out into two feet of snow to take a look around.

I walked along the front of the soddy to the stable, broke the ice in the water trough for the horses, unbuttoned, and wrote my name in the snow. Even without the wind, the cold bit quick and deep, so I didn't dally around outdoors for long. After making a hasty check and finding no tracks close to the house, I edged back through the door and stamped the snow off my boots.

The snap of a cocking pistol turned me into a statue with one foot still hanging in the air. A pair of wide eyes greeted me from Nancy's cot, and I looked down the wrong end of the barrel of my own Navy. Cautiously, I lifted both hands above my head, still holding one foot off the ground. Maybe I saw a sour grin through the darkness, no way to be sure. Anyway, she eased the weapon off cock. The series of tiny clicks sounded clearly in the silence as she spun the cylinder to lower the hammer on the empty chamber again. The Navy and the eyes both vanished under her blankets.

Bobby Nels snapped awake instantly when I touched his shoulder. I spoke close to his ear. "Miss Aldro's a light sleeper, partner. Might be a good idea to tell her if you decide to step outside to do any business. I just got scared gray-headed coming back in the door. Waking a nervous woman who sleeps with a six-gun can give a man a dry mouth and smelly pants."

Bobby snickered, threw aside his blankets, and shuddered when cold air struck him. He slapped on his hat and slipped into his coat before he reached for his boots. The sequence marked him as a Texas drover. I'd heard those boys always dressed from top to bottom. I turned away toward my own bunk to catch a couple more hours of rest. My family dressed in a different order when awakened. We strapped on guns first.

The smell of cooking side meat and boiling coffee brought me back awake. Nancy glanced at me when I appeared in the doorway. "We've been tiptoeing around to let you sleep."

"Thanks. How's your . . . ?" Seeing Aldro's eyes were open, I stopped and addressed the question to him. "How's it going this morning?"

"If being hungry as a bear is a good sign, I'm getting better."

After the meal, Nancy washed the tin plates in a bucket of hot water. Bobby stood by the door, jerked it open when I swung back the bucket, and slammed it shut as soon as the dishwater flew through. That boy moved to get things done without having to be told everything. No need to let in the cold outdoors any more than necessary.

"You going out to pick up Larry?" Aldro's voice sounded stronger.

"Two feet of snow out there. Think I can find him?"

"I owe it to him to ask you to try." Aldro's glance flicked toward Bobby before he added quietly, "I don't like to think about varmints . . ."

"All right. I'll take the wagon."

Bobby said, "I ought to come. He was my brother."

"Your choice to make. I'd rather you stay here. We don't know if there were only two of them. If there are others, and they come after Mr. Aldro while we're gone, with him already sorely wounded, Miss Aldro might be in a fix."

The youngster's eyes lingered on me for a moment while he thought it over. "I'll stay here if you think it best."

"Obliged. I'd feel easier with you here to look after things." No need to hurt his feelings by telling him the truth, that I felt more untroubled riding alone than having a green kid to look after.

His shoulders came back a bit and his jaw set. Jobs such as protecting his wounded boss and a young woman don't make a man feel shorter. Youthful he might be, but Bobby Nels looked determined to shoulder a man's responsibility. If trouble came, he was making up his mind to meet it horn to horn. Come to think of it, my youngest brother was only sixteen when he killed his first three men in about as many seconds. Sometimes the young bulls can be the most dangerous.

Bobby had already fallen in with my practice of sparse talk. He simply lifted a hand when I pulled out after he helped me hitch the team. Aldro's directions led me to the general area where Larry Nels fell. I drove back and forth across the site until the team snorted and shied in the traces, telling me where the body lay under the snow.

At times like this, I gave thanks for being gifted with great strength. I lifted the frozen body easily and placed it gently on the bed of the wagon.

The trip back seemed shorter than coming out. All I had to do was follow the ruts in the snow. Bobby stepped out to meet me when I reined in. He stood for a few moments with his gloved hand on his brother's head. Then he said, "We'll bury him just like he fell. No need to clean him up to put him in the ground."

I went through the pockets and handed Bobby the few odds and ends his brother had been carrying. Without a word, I motioned to a place on the south side of a small rise. He nodded, and I walked to the spot and started to work with a pick. Nobody I'd ever seen could handle this kind of work better than I. The pick cracked sharply against a crust of frozen ground before finding softer soil. Bobby helped with the shovel.

We worked in silence except once when Bobby stopped and leaned against the shovel to rest. He said, "I never figured a judge to be handy like you. Larry'd laugh if he knew such an important man worked so hard for him."

I met his eyes. "I wish I'd known him. I wish I'd heard him laugh."

His face twisted briefly. "You'd have liked him, Judge. Most everybody did."

Two hours' work and the grave was ready.

"Marker?"

He shook his head. "I'll always remember where he is. There's nobody else to care."

"No way to make a box for him, but we could wrap him in a blanket."

"Larry wouldn't like to waste a good blanket. We've always been poor folks. My daddy only had one good suit. He told my mama not to bury it with him, to give that suit to one of the boys. We're not given to wasting things."

We eased the body into its final place.

"Maybe the Aldros would like to pay their respects."

He shook his head again. "No call to get a wounded man and a woman out in this cold."

"If you don't mind, I'd like to read from the Book."

MYNDERSE LIBRARY
31 Fall Street
Seneca Falls, New York 13148

"I'd be obliged. Larry never paid much attention to things like that, but he'd appreciate it."

When I finished and slipped the Book back into my coat, he said simply, "Good-bye, Larry. You were a good brother, and I loved you." He booted the shovel deep into the pile and dropped the first dirt into the grave. Keeping his face turned away, he said, "I'll do this by myself if you don't mind, Judge."

I walked the short distance to the house. When I called out, Nancy lifted the bar and swung the door open. "I saw you digging. Is the grave ready, Luke?"

"The burying's finished. He didn't want you or your dad out in the cold, and he wanted to do the covering by himself."

She had a cup of coffee poured and waiting for me by the time my coat hit a peg in the wall. I sat on Bobby's box to sip my coffee, and she stood like a statue in front of me until I looked up at her.

"You should remember having to bury a good man when you go to bed tonight. You must put your mind to seeing the right side of things."

"Ma'am?"

"You should remember they killed Bobby's big brother without giving him a chance. They were vicious killers. Just put your mind on what they did and what a fine thing it is that you stopped them. Rejoice that they can't do it again to somebody else. Go to sleep thinking about that."

She turned away. I thought for a moment she'd finished. But she hooked a three-legged stool with her foot and swung it into position in front of me. She sat down, smoothed her skirts, and leaned forward a bit to look me in the eye.

"Think about Bobby trying to take on men like that to avenge his brother. They'd just kill him too. Bobby saw one of them clearly. He would've tried to pay a blood debt if he ever saw that man again."

I sat there blinking.

"It takes hard, fierce men to make some things right. Put your mind on the fact that it's God's grace you're made the way you are. You think about what might have happened if a soft, peaceful man had been on that wagon with me when those men rode up. If you want to have bad dreams, dream about that, and be glad you're fast and tough."

"You think I have nightmares?"

She gave me such a look of disgust I lifted a hand as if to stop her from striking me.

"All right. You just seem to have an odd way of knowing things, ma'am."

"There's nothing odd about having good eyesight. It took no special power to see the pain on your face last night."

"And you figured out where the pain came from?"

"Am I wrong?"

I shrugged. She'd figured it out by simple observation and clear thinking. I'd have felt like a fool trying to deny it.

"If I'm right about that, I'm probably right about the other."

"What other, Nancy?"

"Your expression during our train ride. At first, I thought it was the rigid expression of a harsh, cruel man. Now I think it covered sadness. Did a friend or a member of your family die recently?"

I shook my head.

She said quietly, "Then it has to be a woman."

Aldro grunted as he struggled to a sitting position. She darted to him and helped move his wounded leg so he could sit on the edge of his cot. He asked, "You pour all the coffee into that giant over yonder?"

She poured a cup for him, and he looked through his thick brows at me. "Runs in the women in my family, Baynes. Her grandmother, her mother, and now her. They see into people. Used to give me goose pimples. Plays hell with a man's privacy, don't it?"

I held out my cup for another shot of coffee.

Aldro's voice was gentle. "I been listening, couldn't help it. Up to now, I got no complaints, girl. That about bad dreams sounded good to me, sounded helpful. A man who's done right shouldn't lose his sleep over having shot straight. But that last part, about a woman, that sounded like prying."

"No need for her to pry, Aldro. It's not a big secret. I got infatuated with a pretty lady in New York, but she couldn't see anything but my bad points. It's a grief come late in life for me. Most men have been through it several times by the time they reach my age, but I was always a slow child. I didn't walk until I was seven. Didn't talk until I was ten."

Aldro chuckled, his daughter giggled, and I laughed with them.

Nancy said, "I believe that part about not talking."

"I talk," I said defensively. "I just blabbed out my dark secret about unrequited love. What more do you want from a man with a broken heart?"

She gave me her straight look. "I do believe you're starting to recover."

"I said I was slow, Missy, not disabled."

At his tap on the door, I lifted the bar to let Bobby come in. He shed his hat and coat and stood beside the stove, rubbing his hands. "I want to thank you, Judge, for all your help."

"My privilege. Finished already?"

"No, sir. Not yet. Just came in to get out of the cold for a minute."

Aldro said quietly, "Your brother rode for the brand."

That was the first time I heard that expression. Later, I found out that no soul can achieve a higher commendation to the Almighty from a Texas cattleman. Angels in heaven have a horse saddled and ready for a man who rides for the brand.

Bobby Nels's voice trembled for the first time when he said, "When I go back out, I'll tell Larry you said that, Mr. Aldro." A tear escaped to mark a track down his cheek. Nancy turned away and busied herself with something. Aldro lowered his head to stare at the dirt floor. I rocked my cup and fascinated myself with a coffee whirlpool.

FIFTEEN

ALDRO TURNED TO ME. "When are you going back to Cheyenne?"

"I better head back tomorrow. Marshal Lorimer probably has a jail full of Saturday night drunks. I'm a day late now."

"We'll be riding with you."

"Good. Might be a good idea to have the doctor in town look at those wounds of yours. You can ride in my wagon."

Bobby asked, "You want me to stay here and watch after things, Mr. Aldro?"

"I wouldn't ask any man to stay out here alone after having this kind of trouble," Aldro said quietly. "You come with us. I'm needed back in Texas, and I never intended for my daughter to come out here anyhow. I'll hire a couple of local men to look after this place. I'll need your help on the gather, and you know the trail for the drive back up here in the spring."

That little speech told me all I needed to know about how the stiff-necked Aldro bossed men. With a few offhand words, he'd justified pulling young Bobby out of potential danger by making out that he needed the kid too much elsewhere. His tone carried no hint he might be talking to a confused, mournful lad. He spoke as an owner reserving a trail-hardened top hand for more important work.

There remained little to do until the next morning. Under fading starlight, Bobby used a goodly portion of a stack of cut hay to pad the bed of the wagon. I hitched the team, saddled Aldro's horse, and rigged the other horses on a lead line. Snow squeaked like a rusty hinge at every footstep. We threw Bobby's saddle into the wagon, loaded Aldro, and started out at first light.

Hardly any wind stirred the loose snow, and we soon rode through an eye-bleaching bright world under a cloudless sky. The below-zero cold laid a quiet, numbing grip on me, but it didn't provoke the same sense of desperation without the razor-sharp wind we'd faced on the ride out. An hour before noon, I was near frozen in the saddle, so I switched places with Bobby, who'd been riding on the wagon seat with Nancy. By midday, I figured we were making such poor time we'd likely be after dark getting to town.

I hollered at Bobby, and he pulled abreast of the wagon. "Breaking trail in the snow slows the team too much. What say we throw your saddle on a horse? You lead half the horses and I'll lead the other half. We'll ride in front of the wagon to break a trail."

He nodded and Nancy stopped for me to climb down. Bobby grabbed his saddle and had it on one of the horses in about two minutes. It took another minute or two to divide the stock and rig the lead lines. With us riding ahead and breaking through the snow for her team, Nancy picked up a better pace. Aldro shouted from the wagon bed, "We getting close to where you shot those two outlaws?"

"Yeah, somewhere along here, I think. With the snow covering this prairie, it's hard to tell. It's like trying to remember exactly where I dropped something in a lake."

"You plan to pick them up, take the bodies to town?"

"You lonesome? You want to share your wagon with them, Aldro?"

"No, I'll pass on that pleasure, but I'd like to take a look at them. I'd like to know for sure they're the ones who shot me and Larry."

"They'll keep. I'll come after them tomorrow with the marshal, if he's interested. When we get them back to town, you can take a look."

We pulled up in front of the doctor's house at dusk. I trotted up the path to knock on the door while Nancy and Bobby helped Aldro down from the wagon.

Doctor Jordan greeted me with a suspicious eye, looked over my shoulder at Aldro being helped toward the house, and asked crisply, "What did you do to this one?"

"A couple of men shot Mr. Aldro and killed one of his hands. Aldro's pretty weak. He got hit three times."

Jordan nodded and lifted his voice. "Jeremy!" Pitts appeared in the doorway leading to the examining room. "Get your coat. Go get the marshal." When I lifted a brow, he added, "Lorimer likes to know when people get shot around here."

Pitts, moving cautiously to favor his sore ribs, reached for his coat and flashed a grin at me. "Howdy, Judge."

"You still hanging around?"

Doc Jordan answered for him. "He's been helping out around the place." He flipped a hand toward the door to the examining room and said, "Come in here, Mr. Aldro," and led the way. As soon as we got Aldro comfortable on the table, Jordan glanced at me and said, "Wait in the other room." He caught Bobby's eye and jerked his head toward the door, indicating the comment went for him too. At Nancy's questioning expression, he told her, "You can stay."

I leaned over Aldro to meet his eye. "I'll try to get rooms for you, your daughter, and Bobby at the hotel."

He answered shortly, "Good."

Bobby, spread like a bat over the stove, nodded when I said, "If you'd take the horses to the livery, I'd be obliged. Tell the hostler I'll bring the team and wagon back after we get Mr. Aldro to a hotel, if I can get rooms." He buttoned his coat, and we stepped back out into the cold evening together.

The clerk didn't blink when I asked for three rooms. Around a toothpick, he said, "I got two rooms available. I'll have to check on the third one. A couple of partners told me they'd just as soon share a room if we got crowded. I'll ask if they're still willing to double up and let you know."

"How late does the dining room stay open?"

"When I tell that drunken brawler we got for a cook the judge is coming, he'll keep it open all night. He knows when to act friendly."

"Thanks." I mounted Aldro's horse and headed back to Doc Jordan's house.

Marshal Lorimer greeted me with a broad smile when I stepped into the waiting room. "The Aldros tell me you had a full weekend, Judge. You better rent that wagon for another day if we got bodies to bring in tomorrow."

"Not me. You use your money if you want to rent a wagon. Judges' money is for other things. Lawmen like you fool around with corpses. Judges like me don't do that kind of work."

Lorimer cackled and said, "That's so most of the time but, hell, you killed them. You're duty bound to help bring them in."

"Wrong. I just shot them. I didn't adopt them."

He shook his head in mock sorrow. "You're a hard man, Judge Baynes. All right, I'll rent the wagon, and I'll get your story about what happened during our ride out there in the morning. I'll meet you at the hotel for breakfast." He shook hands and walked to the door. Hand on the knob, he turned shrewd, hard eyes on me. "That Aldro girl drew it out mighty plain. You did some fast and fancy gun work, Judge. Most men can throw a pistol straighter than they can shoot it." He ducked out without waiting for an answer.

Nancy said from the door, "The doctor says we can go now. Daddy's wounds are healing fine, but he says he's worn down to a nub and dying from starvation."

When I helped him from the examining table, Aldro asked, "You got us a place to stay?"

"Yeah." I held his coat for him.

"Where?"

"Down at the stable."

"At the stable?" Aldro sounded grim.

"I could only get one stall, so it'll have to do for all of you. It should be cozy. The hostler's shoveling it out for you now. I paid him a dollar for the favor. He said he'd spread some hay soon's he finishes. You don't mind a little horse smell, do you?"

Nancy asked, "Couldn't you find a hotel room?"

"Seems like we went through this before when we got to town late on the train. Remember?"

"Yes." For once, the feisty front wore thin and Nancy sounded glum and tired.

After the short ride to the hotel, we assisted Aldro to a seat in the dining room. I said, "Bobby, help me unload my stuff from that wagon out front." We stacked the stuff in the storeroom behind the hotel desk. He hesitated but made no comment when I plucked the Aldros's baggage off with the other gear. I offered to flip a coin to see which of us would return the horses and wagon to the stable and walk back to the hotel.

Bobby gave me a startled look. "But we'll need the wagon to take Mr. Aldro down there, won't we?"

I gave him a slow shake of my head and a wink. When he caught on, Bobby Nels broke out in a delighted grin. The gray, strained expression dropped away, and I realized I was seeing him smile for the first time since his brother's death.

"No need for coin flipping. I'll take care of the horses. Don't tell them nothin' before I get back. Keep stringing them along." He darted for the door before I could answer.

When I rejoined the Aldros, both of them could hardly hold their eyes open. After a hard day exposed to the penetrating cold, the cozy warmth of the dining room lulled them both to the point they sat staring emptily into space.

Nancy's head snapped up when I pulled back my chair and sat down. Aldro stirred, blinking like he'd just come out of a trance. "Bobby just ran over to the stable, wanted to be sure the shoveling was coming along good. He figured you might be ready to retire after dinner."

She opened her eyes real wide a couple of times and yawned behind her hand. "I'm exhausted. I'll bet you're worn out too, Daddy, with your wounds and that long ride today."

Aldro said gruffly, "I've had better days."

Nancy shot me a pleading glance. "That stable is going to be terribly cold. We can't even make a fire in there. Would you consider letting Daddy share your room? I'm really worried about him."

"I thought the doctor said he was healing fine."

"Well, yes, but he's still very weak from loss of blood. He could get an infection or catch a fever."

"Now, now," I said. "We mustn't coddle him. That would just delay his full recovery."

Bobby burst in, breathing heavily, and hung his coat and hat on a wall peg. At Nancy's questioning look, he said, "Uh, I ran back from the stable. I didn't want my food to get cold."

"How was the shoveling going?" I asked.

"Shoveling? Oh yeah, uh, he'd just started. Said he'd have everything ready in a couple of hours, maybe."

Aldro asked with a gritty voice, "What was that, Nels? A couple of hours? Maybe?"

"Yes, sir. Uh, he said he was going home to eat first, but he'd get started on it again soon's he got back. I'd've gone to work on the job myself, but I figured you wouldn't want me to miss out on my grub either. Lot of stuff in there. They must not clean stalls much when it's this cold."

I nodded solemnly. "I'd help, but I'm a little tired myself, and I hate shoveling after a big meal."

Aldro rubbed his eyes and glanced at Nancy. "I think I'm going to remember today for a long time."

She fixed that straight look of hers on me and said, "That's it. That's the end of it. I'm so tired I haven't been paying attention. That's the absolute end of it, Judge Luke Baynes."

Innocently I asked, "End of what?"

"I've been half asleep or I'd have caught on before. You're lying. You haven't said a truthful word in the last hour."

"Me? Lying? Lying about what?"

"Everything." She put on a prissy expression and said, " 'I hate shoveling after a big meal.' That remark was just too cute. It was a dead giveaway." She shifted her gaze and blasted Bobby with her double-barreled stare. "And you too, you're in on it."

He squirmed like a snared rabbit and mumbled, "Who? Me? In on what?" Wildly looking for escape, his eye caught movement when the door swung open from the kitchen. "Here comes our grub."

The cook unloaded steaming plates he'd stacked up his arm like a circus juggler. I leaned forward to inspect the inch-thick slab of beef covering my plate. "Hey, look at that wee steak. This your lady's day special?"

"If you're still hungry after you eat that, I'll fix you another steak just like that one, but it'll be free." He slapped me on the shoulder and marched back into his domain.

Aldro said, "Looks like you've made a friend in the kitchen."

"Drunks and judges get to know each other quickly. They both have to hang around courtrooms a lot."

The room clerk took that moment to walk in with a big smile. "Here's the key to that third room you wanted, Judge." He slapped it on the table beside my plate, nodded politely to the Aldros, and went back to his desk.

Aldro straightened and stared at the key. He asked, "What's that? Rooms?"

Nancy stared at me and said, "You ought to be shot. I didn't think you were up to pulling such foolishness." She turned to her father and said, "Daddy, Judge Luke Baynes is a lying, flea-bitten, mangy lobo wolf." She shifted her gaze to young Nels. "And he's given fleas and mange to this smirking little coyote."

Aldro rubbed his face to cover a grin. "A joke like this puts a man to thinking about revenge."

I turned on Bobby. "See there. I knew I shouldn't have let you talk me into it. Your little joke went and made them mad."

SIXTEEN

THE NEXT MORNING, Marshal Ben Lorimer sat down and helped me eat the kitchen empty. He took a last sip of coffee and leaned back with a big grin, patting his stomach with a reddened, chapped hand. "That's the way to start a day right."

I nodded.

A look of shock crossed his face. His hand jumped from one pocket of his coat to another. "Uh oh, now that's embarrassing as hell. I must have left my wallet in my other coat."

"Never mind. Be my guest, Marshal."

He beamed and relaxed. "That's a kindness, Judge. I thank you. I've got to pick up a few items yet. Why don't I meet you at the stable in a few minutes?"

"Good. I'll see you there."

Lorimer managed to be just late enough to avoid helping me and the hostler hitch the team in the biting cold. I had joined the hostler next to the stove in the tiny livery stable office when Lorimer finally appeared. I almost failed to recognize him in a buffalo robe and woolly chaps, with a wolf-skin cap pulled down over his ears. He carried a store-bought broom in one mittened hand.

We walked out to the wagon together. He flipped a couple of blankets from under his arm onto the seat and dropped his broom into the bed. "This is the prettiest country in the world in the summer, but the winters make you pay for it. I hope you had the sense to shoot those two horse thieves close to town. You bring something to eat?"

"Not for you. I didn't take you to raise, you tightwad. Don't they pay marshals?"

"Not as much as they pay judges." He glanced back at the bundle on the wagon bed behind the seat. The cook at the hotel had wrapped a flour sack around the food he'd prepared for me and the marshal. With a sly grin, Lorimer said, "Looks like enough for both of us."

I snapped the reins to start the team. It took five minutes to tell Lorimer the whole story about the shooting. Then I settled back and fell into my usual habit of silence on the trail.

My uneasiness about having a difficult time locating the bodies under the snow turned out to be a needless worry. In fact, I'd rather have had trouble finding them. We could tell from a hundred yards away that wolves had discovered them first.

The horses plunged and bucked in the traces, so I headed them around the site in a wide arc. When I pulled them to a halt, facing upwind, Lorimer said, "Stay on the wagon and hold the horses."

He dismounted and circled the bodies, scanning the snow, forevermore looking like a huge, shaggy hound searching for a scent. I sat and watched a different side of Lorimer come into view. The relaxed, comfort-seeking man vanished. The man I watched now moved slowly, almost painfully patient, checking every track in the snow. The lawman appeared to be memorizing every detail of the scene.

Finally, he squatted a few feet from one of the bodies, studying the grisly red stains scattered all around him. Several minutes passed while his head swung slowly back and forth. Then he rose, used his broom to brush the body clean of snow, and rolled the corpse over. Again, several minutes passed while he stared as if committing everything to memory. Then he went through the clothing and put the contents of the dead man's pockets in a small cloth bag. He repeated the deliberate procedure when he approached the second body.

At his wave, I fought the team until they danced and fidgeted beside the closest remains. He said, "Hold that damn team. I don't need any help." He lifted the heels of the first frozen corpse and propped them against the rear of the wagon. Then he grabbed the shoulders and heaved the body forward. The remains slid onto the wagon like a knotty log. After doing the same with the second one, he flipped a blanket more or less over the bodies, climbed aboard, and mutely pointed south toward Cheyenne.

I had hardly got the horses moving before he asked plaintively, "Aren't you hungry yet?" I gave him a sour look and he shrugged, the gesture almost lost under the shaggy buffalo robe. "Now don't go milky-faced on me, Judge. Just a couple of dead men. No call to get edgy."

"I never saw anybody chewed by wolves before."

Lorimer shrugged again. "Hell, everybody gets hungry out in this cold. I don't see why wolves should be any different from everybody else." He snared the flour sack. "Let's see what we got here."

Moments later, chewing contentedly, he asked idly, "Did you say that Aldro girl shot one of those fellows first?"

"No. I said we shot close together."

"Oh yeah, that's right. She's the one said she shot first." He took another huge bite and chewed in silence for awhile. "A little thing like that, now, I guess it don't ordinarily make any difference. I got it figured you shot first though."

"How did you figure that?"

"That frozen wolf bait riding behind us used to be brothers. I know both of 'em. There are two more boys in that trashy family, and their daddy strikes me to be about as mean as a grizzly with a bellyache. Name's Dorcas. Never could tell those boys apart. They're like as peas in a pod, all of 'em rat-faced ugly. All of 'em figure they're genuine hard cases. They're likely to have hard feelings."

"So?"

"Two things. First, you keep your eyes peeled if anybody named Dorcas comes around. If you see one, figure at least one of the others is close by. Second, I wouldn't want them coming after that girl. That's a bad thought, isn't it, what with her daddy wounded and all? That's why it was a relief to me just now when you said you shot first." He paused and stared off into the distance before he asked quietly, "That's what you said, wasn't it, Judge?"

"Yeah, now that I think back on it, that's right."

"Good. Women tend to get flighty in troubled times. They aren't steady like men. I figured that Aldro child was confused when she said she shot first. Must have been a terrible thing for a sweet little thing like her to go through. Probably scared her half to death. A grown man is more likely to have the straight of it. Isn't that a fact?"

Poker-faced, I glanced at him. "Lots of people feel that way."

Equally poker-faced, he said, "That's dead right. If folks want to believe a certain way, it's surefire to cause an upset if some fool tries to change their minds. Now then, the way this falls out, those boys came at you, and you killed them both. No doubt about it. Right, Judge?"

I nodded. "No need to cause an upset."

"Yeah, you got the idea. You might talk to Miss Aldro. She told me she shot one of those boys before you did. I figure she was, uh, distraught when she talked to me, what with all that excitement and her worried about her daddy and all such as that. I figured she meant to say she wanted to shoot him."

He deliberately pulled the cuffs of his coat and smoothed his sleeves, letting that complicated job draw his total attention. He spoke slowly, spacing each word as if he'd picked it with great care.

"You get her calmed down so she says it right. Lots of difference between wanting to do something and doing it. I figure she did want to shoot him. Right, Judge? It just makes a better story if you shot them both, that being the straight truth anyway. Besides, folks would be shocked to see a pretty little thing like that even carry a pistol, never mind shoot it."

He stretched his legs and stamped his cold feet, making the skittish horses surge forward. Ignoring my problem trying to control the jittery team, he hawked and spat juicily. "Sure makes my job easier, having a judge involved in this incident. A man trained in the law sees things real clear and doesn't forget what's important." He reached into the flour sack again. "You sure you aren't hungry, Judge?"

We rode in silence for the rest of the trip back to Cheyenne. Lorimer came along with me to drop off the wagon and team after we unloaded the grisly cargo at the undertaker's. Six or eight men stood around the corral when we arrived.

The hostler tilted his head toward the group and said, "The boys are looking over some new stock before it gets too dark. I just traded today for half a dozen Indian blanket horses, Judge. Got some really good stock, and you're just in time to buy a good animal before the best ones are all gone. You might be interested in buying a horse too, Marshal."

I said solemnly, "The marshal's too broke to buy his own lunch. Are they broken to the saddle?"

"More or less, but they ain't ladies' horses. They're still

barefoot, but I'll pay to have the animal shod if you decide to buy one."

I put on an uninterested expression and answered in an offhand tone. "I'll take a look."

Two of the men standing around the corral nodded when we joined them. Lorimer said, "Gentlemen, meet Judge Luke Baynes. You boys see anything good?" They offered their names and shook hands.

One of them said, "It depends on what a man likes, I guess. Most everybody is satisfied with a good mustang, but I've always admired an Appaloosa. Generally, they got a nice shape."

The hostler stepped into the corral and approached the horses. He shook out a rope and started them into a trot around the fence. The gathered men moved forward to watch each animal closely as it passed. After about two minutes of listening to their comments, I knew the group included nobody with a serious intention to buy. Nobody praises a horse he really wants, not unless he's got so much money it tires him to carry it around.

A big, rangy red gelding with a "blanket" of gray spots covering his rump and another across his shoulders caught my eye. Frisky and light on his feet, he ran with his head high, unafraid of the man but running anyway just for the fun of it, showing a lot of white around the eyes in the way of his kind. A big gray in the group had the size I wanted to carry my weight, but he showed little spirit, tended to stop and stand with head lowered at every chance. I gestured at the gray. "Put a rope on that one. I'd like to take a look at him."

"Nice, calm horse," the hostler said when he led the animal to me.

After a careful inspection, I asked, "What do you want for this one?"

He named a price, and I grimaced. After pretending to give it thought, I shook my head sadly and said, "I sure like him, but I guess he's too much horse for me. I better try to pick one you're not so proud of."

I picked another, and the hostler roped him. The price for this one started out a little lower, but I gave another pained look and shook my head. We dickered for awhile. The other men wandered off. The sun set and darkness started to close in on us. "He's surely worth it. I know that, but I just can't afford that good a horse, I guess. Thanks for your trouble."

I took a couple of steps away and paused. Over my shoulder, using a disappointed voice, I asked, "What about that big red? He's got a skittish look, but maybe I could spend some time with him and get him to calm down some."

He pulled his watch and took a close look at it in the fading light. "Want me to rope him for you, Judge?"

"No, I guess I'm keeping you from your supper."

"No trouble at all. Won't take a minute." He was right. About a minute later, he led the red to me. The big horse snuffled curiously at my coat.

"He's kind of a plug after looking at those others, isn't he? But a man of limited means can't have everything he wants."

Lorimer said, "Maybe you finally picked one you can afford, Judge."

The hostler gave him a poisonous glance.

"How much for this one?"

"Hell, Judge, that's the best of the lot."

Lorimer snickered and got himself another venomous glance.

My doubtful smile fixed on my face, I said, "You don't think he'd shy at every little thing? He looked pretty wild out in the corral."

"Ain't nothin' wrong with that horse. I tell you, he's the pick of the lot."

"Well, I do thank you for your trouble."

"Now wait a minute, Judge. Don't go walking off when a

man is talking to you." He named a fair price for the first time since we'd started talking. Then he pulled his watch again, his expression stoic. I could almost hear his wife giving him a scorching opinion of men who came late to supper.

Darkness shrouded Cheyenne by the time I bought a big red horse, with a week's free feed and a new bridle thrown in. The hostler shook hands on the deal with the same enthusiasm as a gambler throws in a second best hand.

After we'd walked halfway to the hotel, Lorimer said, "First time since I pinned on a badge I've done a thing like that."

"Like what?"

"Like standing there like a post and watching a judge steal a horse. Makes a man lose his faith. Can't trust anybody anymore. Preachers are born with their hands out, every one of 'em, but I thought judges had a conscience."

"It got dark. You can swear you couldn't see."

"I'll keep quiet if you'll treat me to dinner."

"Listen to him. What about me keeping quiet about you helping me? That remark about me finally picking a horse I can afford didn't hurt anything. Besides, it's your turn, for heaven's sake. I bought lunch for both of us, and you ate it all, every crumb. I just remembered. I bought breakfast too."

"Yeah, but I did all the heavy work cleaning up your mess. You just sat up on the wagon, hands folded, keeping your skirts tucked in and looking prim."

"Don't try to pull that. You told me to hold the team. Besides, I was doing your job in the first place. Marshals are supposed to shoot outlaws. Judges don't go in for that rough stuff."

He extended both mitten-covered hands, palm up. "Have I acted small about it? Not me. A less generous man would be grieved about you interfering in my work like that. Not me. I'm just not the kind to gripe and find fault. You made a mess, and I cleaned it up. That's a fact. Seems little enough to buy a man's dinner, a man who's so helpful, a man who never complains, a man who . . ."

"All right, I give up."

SEVENTEEN

ALDRO, NANCY, and young Bobby waved when we walked into the dining room. I shook my head at their invitation to join them and pulled out a chair at an adjoining table.

Marshal Lorimer and I had eaten our way through our first steaks and started on the second when Bobby excused himself and walked out. The two Aldros picked up their coffee cups and shifted places to sit with us. Nancy looked at our plates and asked, "Are you another one, Marshal? I didn't know there were two men in the world who ate like four."

I said, "She's not used to seeing real men eat. She's never been around anything but Texans before now."

Lorimer nodded solemnly and said, "I see," like that explained everything.

Aldro said, "Just keep on, Baynes. I'm making a list. When I get well, you'll answer for all of this."

A small man appeared at the marshal's elbow. "I just saw the bodies you brought in, Marshal. What happened?"

Lorimer looked up and put on a sour expression. "I'm eating."

The man looked around the table and said, "I'm Jedediah Jacobson, editor of the best newspaper in Cheyenne."

Lorimer said sullenly, "The only newspaper in Cheyenne."

Jacobson asked, "What happened?"

"I'm eating," Lorimer said again.

"The public has a right to know. I need a statement from you."

The marshal said, "If the public had a right to know, they'd have put that in the Constitution, and publishing a newspaper would be part of my job. Right, Judge?" He stuffed a chunk of beef into his mouth.

The little man's eyes flicked briefly at me, but I ignored the question. He stood patiently while the marshal chewed.

Finally, Lorimer swallowed and said with a tired voice, "I'll look you up first thing in the morning. No, it'll be the second thing in the morning. I want to let my breakfast settle first." He paused, rubbed his forehead, and winked at me from behind his hand so Jacobson couldn't see. "On second thought, why don't you meet me here and buy my breakfast? That way I won't lose any time from my job."

Jacobson said, "I'm told the dead men are two of that Dorcas bunch. That means whoever shot them is probably in serious trouble. Do you know who did it?"

When Lorimer acted as if he hadn't heard the question, Jacobson said evenly, "All right, I'll see you in the morning." He turned to me. "Are you Judge Lucas Baynes, sir?"

"Luke Baynes. The name is Luke." I rose as he stepped forward to shake hands.

"I'd like a few minutes of your time too, Judge. I'd like to have a little background, where you're from, that sort of thing."

"Well, if you're standing treat for breakfast, I wouldn't want to miss it."

He took a long, slow breath, and opened his mouth to speak. A glance at Nancy stopped him. His mouth clamped shut in a straight line. Finally, with an obvious effort, he said quietly, "Very well, gentlemen." He spun on his heel and marched out.

Lorimer sighed and placed his fork carefully on his plate. "I do believe that little fellow barely stopped himself from using unseemly language."

I said innocently, "Odd, wasn't it?"

Nancy said, "You both should be ashamed. That poor little man."

Lorimer shrugged. "I hate writers. It's amazing what a man will do to avoid honest work. I bet he could polish spittoons as good as a full-sized man."

Nancy said, "I take it you don't read much."

"I do, ma'am, I do. But sitting around scribbling all day doesn't seem much for a man to be doing with himself. Maybe it'd be all right if he'd lost a leg or two, or if he was consumptive or something like that. Seems to me he might as well join the ladies and sit around gossiping all day."

She said, "For all the ladies, I thank you."

He rubbed his mouth and said, "I must've stepped in something. My boot tastes terrible."

I said, "That was a bad slip, Marshal. Times are changing. I read the other day that the first woman passed the bar exam in New York. Now we're going to have women lawyers."

"That's good. Don't you think so, Miss Nancy?" Beads of sweat appeared on the marshal's brow.

She smiled and patted Lorimer's hand. "I won't tell the ladies what you said, Marshal." He started to relax. "Until tomorrow morning." He made a pained face, and we all laughed.

Aldro said, "Since you men have finished your meal, maybe I can bring up some business. I think those two men who tried to kill me were after more than horses."

He paused to take a quick look around the empty dining room before he continued. "Larry Nels and I found surveyors on my property a few days ago. They told us they were surveying railroad land for a development company. I told them they were on my property, that I'd already bought the land from the railroad. They told me I'd better check my title."

Aldro turned to me. "I didn't buy until after I met you. Up till now, I just thought their maps might not be up to date back in New York."

"You knew each other before?" Lorimer's brows lifted.

"We met on a fox hunt," I said.

Aldro continued, "It just came to me that somebody might think it was a great idea to try to sell land twice. I made no secret of the fact that I planned to go home, gather a herd, and drive it up here. That's still what I plan to do. If they killed my two hired men, there'd be nobody to let me know anything was going on. By the time I got back up here next summer, I'd find my pasturage plowed up by a hundred farmers."

"Not smart," I said. "The railroad would have to make good."

Aldro shook his head. "They always have somebody else do their dirty work. For example, suppose they sold the land to a middleman. He'd do all the selling to farmers, probably selling mine again and some of the public domain too. Then he'd divide the money with those crooked railroaders and vanish. The railroad could claim it's not their fault. I'd have to drive all kinds of people off my property. It'd probably start the worst range war you ever saw."

Lorimer said, "That's a lot to come up with from just seeing a couple of surveyors."

"Maybe so," Aldro said grimly, "but I'm putting both of you on notice right now. You're the law. When I come back up here next summer with a herd of cattle, I expect to find wide open grassland, not plowed fields."

"I don't know what I can do at this end." Lorimer sounded puzzled. "If they sell the land in New York, that's out of my jurisdiction. Those folks will be flooding out here in the spring with titles. I don't know a good title from a bad one. That's the judge's business."

I put my cup down. "You need somebody on the spot to investigate. I'd suggest you get a lawyer in New York."

Aldro grimaced. "I can't do that again. I'm near broke from hiring one once before." He shot a meaningful glance at me. "New York lawyers cost a fortune."

"You don't need to hire the senior partner in a law firm," I said. "Hire a younger lawyer at one quarter the price."

"How am I going to find a competent man? You know a good man I can afford?"

I met Aldro's eye. "As a matter of fact, I just happen to know a young lawyer I'd trust completely."

"What's this going to cost me?" Aldro asked.

"What's it going to cost you if you don't hire him?"

"I can't go back to New York. I need to get home as soon as I can travel without suffering."

"We have trains and telegraphs these days. Send him a telegram and ask him to come here."

"That'll cost like sin. He'll spend a week on the train just coming here and going back without doing one thing for me."

I nodded. "You can always go on back to Texas and worry about it. It would be a shame to spend all that money just to save a little worrying."

"Who's the lawyer?"

"Young fellow named Roland Sands."

"Try to get him for me, will you?"

"I'll give you an address. You send your own telegram. You can mention I recommended him. It might help persuade him to come all the way out here. I better not get involved beyond that. This whole thing might land in my court."

Aldro turned to Nancy. "Go tell Nels I want him to take a telegram down to the telegraph office for me." His hard gaze came back to me. "You got a crazy sense of humor sometimes, Baynes. This is no joke. This lawyer better be good."

"I have a wonderful sense of humor about everything, Mr.

Aldro. If you ever step into my courtroom guilty of a capital crime, I may laugh you all the way to the gallows."

I guess the remark didn't sound friendly, but I wanted no doubt, not any, not ever, that a man with a sense of humor could do serious work. That comment should also clear any doubts from his mind that he'd bought a puppet judge. He'd bribed a few Tammany Hall politicians, not me.

Nancy left the room to go after Bobby during the silence that followed my little speech.

Lorimer stirred restlessly in his chair and asked, "Why do you suppose those boys didn't stay and finish the job when they tried to kill you?"

Aldro said, "Young Nels might have been a surprise for them. Maybe they only expected to find two men out there."

He pulled at his left sleeve to shift his wounded arm. His face showed the deepened lines of a man growing tired.

"They hung around for a couple of days keeping us penned in the soddy, but then a storm came up. I figure they didn't want to get caught in the open and have to stand up to that kind of punishment. Besides, once they got our horses, they figured they could come back at us anytime they felt like it. Maybe they headed back this way to get more help."

Aldro tilted his head toward me. "They certainly didn't expect to run into anybody like you."

"Or your daughter," I added quietly.

EIGHTEEN

ALDRO'S WOUNDS continued to heal without complication. When the day came, he thought he should come along with us, but Nancy nattered at him so much he agreed to wait at the hotel rather than meet Cotton at the train station.

I said solemnly, "Cotton Sands might be a lot more enthused about the job if the pretty Aldro rather than the grumpy one meets him first. You might get a cheaper deal."

Nancy put on a mocking expression and gave me a deep curtsy. Aldro said, "I'll add that remark to my list I'm keeping on you, Baynes."

Nancy and I walked to the station through the frigid darkness. When we arrived, Jed's wagon sat outside while he enjoyed the indoor comfort of a chair positioned just the right distance from a stove and a spittoon. His weathered face distorted into what he thought was a smile when he looked up and saw Nancy. He rose and said, "Howdy, Miss Aldro."

He dropped back into his chair and squirmed himself comfortable before he got around to noticing me. "You meetin' somebody, Judge?"

"Yeah."

"Want me to go see if Doc Jordan's home? I could have him get things ready if you're gonna send him more trade."

"No, thanks."

"Well, I'm thinking of going into the ambulance and hearse business on the side. You wouldn't mind if I follered you around, would you? A man should go where business is good."

"You need bows and a canvas cover for that wagon if you're going to call it an ambulance."

"Naw, folks out here's used to plain dealing. We know them frills is just to make stuff more expensive anyhow."

"How much, without frills, to take us back to the hotel?"

"You, Miss Aldro, and how many others?"

"One."

"He got baggage?"

"I guess so."

"A dollar."

"Just one dollar? Why did you charge me so much before?"

"You was a stranger then. You're home folks now. You even got a nickname in the saloons."

"You don't say? What do they call me?"

Nancy turned away to stare out the frosted window, but I saw her shut her eyes and grimace.

"You ain't heard about it? Well now, ain't that a good one? The paper came out early this morning. Don't you read?"

I shook my head. "Never had time to learn."

Nancy stared fixedly out the window.

Jed warmed to his job. "Everybody calls you the Wyoming giant. Everybody says we got us a giant judge. It's all over town. Ain't that right, Miss Nancy?"

Nancy studied the railroad tracks through the window.

Jed went on without waiting for an answer. "They says you sleep half crosswise and still stick out at both ends 'cause you're built too long for an ordinary bed. Lots of people hereabouts has high regard for young Jeremy Pitts as a handy fistfighter. You broke a rib and laid him up for a week by poking him with your finger. Ain't that right, Miss Nancy?"

Nancy made a noncommittal humming sound.

Jed nodded. "Sure. Everybody's seen Pitts cripping around town, acting ninety years old. You looked three drunks straight in the eye in your courtroom, and they've done swore off liquor, every single one of 'em. Those boys say you bruised their eyeballs so bad they couldn't work for two days."

I said, "Don't tell me this nonsense was in a newspaper. I don't believe it."

He pointed at my coat. "The paper said it took ten sheep to make that there coat of yours. A body can't keep up with all the stories goin' around. Two Dorcas boys with a tough repu- tation braced you, and you shot both of 'em square through the heart and left 'em for the wolves. Hell, most of it was in the newspaper."

I spoke to Nancy's back, "Did you know about this?"

When she faced me, she managed to smile and look worried at the same time. "It wasn't really quite that bad. Jed's adding to it a little bit. I stole the newspaper in front of your door this morning. I got the clerk to hide all the others around the hotel until you left, so you wouldn't see them."

"Why on earth did you do that?"

"Remember that funny little man you and Marshal Lorimer treated so mean, made him buy your breakfast? He got his revenge. I was afraid you'd get mad and squash him."

"Oh, for heaven's sake, Nancy, I don't squash people."

She snickered. "You really should be nice to writers, Luke. I think it serves you right."

"How come nobody told me anything?"

"Messengers who carry bad news get killed, especially if they bring bad news to mean giants. You're so quiet and stone-faced, people don't rush up to tell you things. Besides, you've been gone most of the day, playing with your new horse."

"Training my new horse, you mean. I been getting him used to the sound of shooting, so he won't be gun-shy. That's work."

"You run off to play with your horse and your guns and call that work?"

I put on my stern judge's face.

She shrugged. "Anyway, you left right after closing the court at noon. When has anybody had a chance to talk to you?"

"You did. Why didn't you tell me?"

"I told you why. I was afraid you'd wad that little man into a ball and throw him through his own plate-glass window."

"I don't get mad that easy."

"You do too. You most certainly do."

A train whistle interrupted a conversation I could tell had reached a dead end anyway.

We waited inside the station, watching the engine ease to a stop in clouds of vapor, lighted car windows opaque with frost except for oddly-shaped splotches where passengers had rubbed spots to see through. I stood behind Nancy while she rubbed the station window with her scarf.

She asked, "What does he look like?"

"Just look for the most handsome man you ever saw."

She threw an impatient glance back at me. "Oh, Luke, be serious."

I threw up both hands. "Further deponent sayeth not."

"What's that mean?"

"Lawyer talk. It means I have nothing more to say."

"Oh, Luke, come on. Describe him and let me see if I can pick him out."

"All right. He'll step down from the car and head for the shadows."

"Really?"

"You just listen to what I tell you."

Passengers stepped down and cringed when struck by the penetrating cold. The dim light of the lantern set out by the ticket agent revealed little more than shapes and shadows unless people walked close to our window. I knew Cotton at once, more by his manner and posture than by being able to see his features or clothing. His slim, erect figure moved into the shadows as soon as he came down the car steps. His bags on the ground, he scanned the station platform with habitual taut alertness.

"He'll straighten his clothing, like a well-dressed man who hates wrinkles. Actually, he'll be getting his guns adjusted to feel just right under his coat."

Cotton jerked gently at his cuffs. Then his hands slid idly down the front of his coat in slow, smoothing motions.

Her voice gone quiet, she said, "That's him, isn't it? He's not very tall. The one moving into the light right now?"

"I didn't say he was big. I said he was good-looking. Now he'll come inside. He'll probably rub an eyebrow with his left hand, or some move like that so it won't be so obvious that he's looking everything over. Look at his eyes. They'll have about as much expression as a Wyoming snowbank."

Cotton stepped inside and put his bags aside with an easy shove. His left hand went to the brim of his hat. He hadn't been inside the room for a full second before he spotted me. A smile sprang to his lips.

Nancy blew out her breath like she'd been holding it too long and squeezed my arm. "Luke, he's beautiful. What a stunning smile."

Cotton walked toward us, extending his hand to shake mine while still four steps away. Actually, he ended up grabbing my hand with both of his. "God, how I've missed you, Rube."

"Same here." I glanced at Nancy. "Miss Nancy Aldro, may I introduce Mr. Roland Sands."

He bowed over the hand she offered. Cotton's eyes flashed at me, and I took a quick glance around us. His expression looked like he was sending a caution signal, but I saw nothing unusual. I raised a brow and gave him a baffled look.

His attention drawn back to Nancy, Cotton said smoothly, "I'm pleased to meet the prettiest lady in Cheyenne, Miss Aldro."

She simpered, and I looked close to make sure this was the same Nancy Aldro I thought I knew. Coyly, she said, "You haven't seen enough to make that kind of judgment, Mr. Sands."

"No need, ma'am. The best way to find the prettiest lady anywhere is to look at the one Judge Baynes has on his arm."

"Really? Isn't that interesting." She looked up at me with an I-told-you-he-was-wonderful smirk.

Cotton grimaced at me as soon as Nancy's attention swerved away from him. He stopped just short of waving his arms.

Mystified about what distressed him, I said, "We've got a wagon, Cotton. The hotel's not far from the station, but we figured you'd have luggage to carry. Besides, nobody comes here really ready for the cold."

He made a big show of being casual. "That's kind of you. I brought my sister. She's waiting in the car to keep warm while I get things ready."

I took quick stock of myself and relaxed. My feelings for Helen hadn't changed, but I could always hide behind my lawyer's face. I vowed that, whatever happened, I'd do nothing to embarrass myself or Helen. I'd play the good sport no matter what the cost. Some things simply must be endured.

"Oh, how wonderful." I had never heard Nancy gush before, and I turned to look at her. She met my surprised glance with a bright smile and said, "We'll keep each other company while you men talk business." I'd never seen her take a backward step from any business discussions. Her straight gaze warned me not to say anything of the sort.

I said, "I didn't know Helen was coming, Cotton. I didn't reserve her a room. Accommodations are tight in Cheyenne, especially for ladies."

"Never mind," Nancy said sweetly. "She can share my room with me. We'll have a wonderful time."

Cotton said, "May I have a word with Judge Baynes, Miss Aldro? Please excuse us." He pulled me aside.

"Damn it, Rube! This is terrible. Helen's been wild since

you left. She's been talking endlessly about coming to Wyoming to find you. When I said I was coming here on business, she was packed in five minutes and leaning against the door. Why did you bring that pretty little thing with you? Helen will scratch her eyes out."

"Think, Cotton. When all else fails you, stop and think. That pretty thing's name is Aldro. Does that ring a bell?"

"I should have caught that. Is she related to my client?"

"Daughter."

"Good. That might delay disaster for about five minutes. You didn't wait long before you found another woman, you rake."

"Just a friend. She's already set her cap for you."

"What are you talking about, Rube? I just got off the damned train."

"Things happen fast out west."

He flinched at a blast from the train whistle. "Oh, God, let's get Helen off that thing before they take her to California." He sprang for the station door.

But Helen entered before he could reach it. She dropped a pair of fat carpetbags to the floor and scanned the room. When her eye found me, she smiled. I'd most nearly forgotten that smile. She ran a hand behind her neck and smoothed her bright hair. She wore a lustrous sable stole.

NINETEEN

HELEN WALKED across the busy room with her eyes fixed on me as if nobody but the two of us existed.

"I've missed you, Luke."

"That's nice to hear," I answered with polite reserve and gestured toward Nancy. "I'd like to introduce Miss Nancy Aldro. Miss Aldro, this is Miss Helen Sands."

Helen's eyes widened as she seemed to notice Nancy for the first time. The two ladies nodded distantly but said nothing.

"Grab your bags, Cotton. I'll bring Helen's. The wagon is right beside the station." I turned to Jed. "We've got one more passenger than I planned."

He shrugged. "Our deal stands. Both ladies can ride up front with me."

I picked up Helen's bags and led the way. Cotton and I sat on the back of the wagon facing to the rear like a couple of barefoot boys, legs dangling. On the way to the hotel, he said, "I hope I don't get spoiled by all this luxury. Does it stay this cold all the time here?"

"Gets warmer in the summer."

Cotton threw up both hands in pretended amazement. " 'Gets warmer in the summer.' Why can't I think of sparkling lines like that? That's a classic bucolic gem if ever I heard one. It also shows deep sympathy from a rube for a friend who's freezing to death."

"The answer was no dumber than the question."

He lowered his voice so they couldn't hear up front. "It's hard to argue when a man's freezing the fixtures off his fanny."

When I didn't reply, he put his hands over his cold ears. "I need a coat like yours." He tilted his head toward Nancy. "And hers."

Cotton turned up his expensive coat collar and stuffed his hands in his pockets. Since we rode the rest of the way in silence, we heard the conversation between the women up front, not that there was much of it.

Helen said, "It's much colder here than in New York. I envy you that lovely warm coat."

Nancy replied, "Luke bought this for me. I just love it."

Helen's reply came after a noticeable pause. "Yes, I see it's almost exactly like the one he's wearing. He has such good taste, doesn't he?"

"Simply wonderful. Practical too."

The conversation stopped right there, and the temperature seemed to drop another twenty degrees.

When we pulled up in front of the hotel, Helen and Nancy trotted in the front door, neither of them showing any inclination to delay in the cold street. I grabbed Helen's bags and told Cotton, "Aldro wants to meet you in the dining room for dinner. As soon as you're settled, come on down. No business tonight, so be sure Helen knows she's welcome to join us. Aldro just wants to size you up."

Cotton, bags in hand, moved quickly up the front steps. "Why did he send all the way to New York for me?"

"Because I lied to him."

"You did what?" In his rush to get away from the cold, he followed me into the lobby, dropped his bags, and almost shut the door in Jed's face. "Oops, pardon me, sir."

Jed ignored him, stepped in, and accepted my dollar. After a silent pause with his hand still extended, he accepted another with a contented expression. "Good night, Judge."

"You still married, Jed?"

He hit the center of the spittoon beside the door and winked. "Man never knows until he comes home of a night. I'll know in a few minutes."

"Thanks, Jed. Good night." I turned back to Cotton as Jed ducked out and closed the front door behind him.

Cotton asked quickly, "You lied to Aldro?"

"Yeah. I told him you were an honest lawyer."

Cotton said, "Did you swear him to secrecy? Rumors like that could get me disbarred."

He signed the register, and we lugged baggage up the stairs. He flung his bags into his room and followed me down the hall toward Nancy's. "Wait for me, Rube. I don't want to miss your dying words."

"What're you talking about?"

"When one or both of them kills you, I'll catch your last words for the history books."

Nancy answered my knock. I dropped Helen's bags inside the door and said, "See you downstairs at your pleasure, ladies." Helen didn't even turn my way from her seat on the bed. Nancy aimed a smile like a rifle right between Cotton's eyes. I shut the door and headed toward my room, Cotton on my heels. He followed me inside and shut the door before he asked casually, "Did you say you had no interest in that Aldro girl?"

"No."

"No?"

"No, I didn't say that at all."

"I thought you did."

"I said we were friends. I take an interest in my friends."

"Friends?"

"That's all."

"No romance?"

"No romance."

He smoothed his coat and looked pleased. "Good-looking woman. Helen will be relieved to hear you aren't interested if we can tell her in time, while that Aldro girl is still alive."

"That Aldro girl has a name. Her name is Nancy. What's this all about? Your sister turned me down, Cotton. I'm just getting to where I can handle that without a bad limp. Why'd you bring her out here?"

He shrugged. "She changed her mind about you. Women do that, you know, Rube. I'll talk real slow so you can write that down and not forget it. You ready?" He spoke with exaggerated slowness: "Women change their minds. Got it? Did I go too fast for you?"

"That's hard to believe."

"I never lie to the simpleminded." He plopped himself into my only chair. "All she did for days was stagger around and cry every time I looked at her. I said some clever things about her lack of intelligence, but that didn't seem to make her feel better."

He sailed his hat, hooking it perfectly to the top of one of my bedposts, looked at me, and made a sour mouth. "Mother Belle was devastating, Rube. God, that's a tough old woman. She said vicious things to Helen, all in the sweetest, most sympathetic voice you ever heard. She said that some women didn't know how to enjoy a full-blooded man, and it was odious for such a man to be wasted, there being pitifully few of them."

Cotton slid down in my chair and laced his fingers together over his stomach. He spoke mechanically, as if reciting lines from memory. "Some women only have the courage to marry pathetic men who will give them short, narrow-shouldered sons, men who ensure that they lead safe, perfectly dull, stodgy lives. Meek women seek tame men. They do it because they'd gag and spew if they tasted the spice of life."

He rubbed his face and then brushed idly at his coat. "I wanted to run and hide. That's a wicked-tongued old woman. I never heard anything like it. All the time she talked, she rocked away in her creaky old chair, back and forth, back and forth, all maternal sweetness and understanding, looking old enough to have tempted Adam."

I asked, "You coming to dinner smelling like you do?"

"What?" Cotton bolted upright.

"You want to clean up a bit before we eat?"

"Yeah. I guess I better do that. Time passes. I'll see you downstairs." He came to his feet and walked out, came right back in, grabbed his hat off my bedpost, and left again.

I considered changing for dinner, decided against it, changed my mind, and put on a clean shirt. I checked my Navy and wondered if Nancy intended to keep its twin forever. Then I peered into the mirror, decided to trim my beard, searched for the scissors, couldn't find them, and decided to hell with it. I went downstairs.

Aldro sat alone, drinking coffee. He'd had the cook put two tables together. I sat down with my back to the kitchen, so I could face the door to the lobby. "Your lawyer and I will have female companionship at dinner. You're odd man out, Aldro."

"I hear you. I got a wife in Texas, and I'm feeling the urge to travel."

"You must be feeling better. What's Doc Jordan say? You up to the trip?"

"Never occurred to me to ask him. Think I should?"

"Seems to be a pretty good doctor."

"Yeah. I was already healing and getting stronger when I met him. He didn't make me worse. That must mean he's better than most."

Marshal Ben Lorimer walked in and looked around the empty dining room. "Howdy, Judge, Mr. Aldro. You folks eating late today? We got things to talk about. Mind if I join you?"

Aldro gestured toward a chair. He grinned when I sent him a warning glance. I wondered which of us would end up paying for the marshal's meal.

Helen and Nancy walked in at that moment, Cotton trailing along behind. I made the introductions. As soon as everyone was seated, Lorimer said blandly, "Jethro Dorcas and his other two boys came to town to pick up the bodies today."

When nobody said anything, he continued, "Dorcas didn't allow as how he could believe one man could shoot down both of his boys in any kind of a fair fight. He spouted war talk. Said just because you were a judge didn't put you above paying for what you did, didn't give you any special rights. I'd watch my step from now on, Judge."

Helen looked at me, eyes wide in a shocked expression.

"Special rights? Two men shot down? What's he talking about?"

Caught flat-footed, I told the unvarnished truth. "We had some trouble a few days ago. I shot a couple of men named Dorcas."

She asked in a horrified tone, "You shot two men? You killed two men?"

The tone of her voice grated on me, and I felt heat come to my face. She sounded like she was accusing me of running naked down the street, scandalizing all decent people. Any time a man feels anger rise in him, he should stop and think before he speaks. I didn't this time. I said flatly, "Graveyard dead. I stopped what I was doing at the time to check them both very carefully to be sure."

Helen came to her feet, but Nancy was up just as quickly. "Please keep your seat, Miss Sands."

"I think I've heard enough."

Nancy pointed at Helen's chair and said sharply, "Nonsense. You haven't heard half enough."

"I resent your tone of voice, Miss Aldro."

Nancy said, "Sit back down. Sit down right there, right now, or I'll pull your hair out."

"How dare you? Just who do you think you are?"

Nancy glanced at me and said, "I see your problem, Luke. She really is a ninny."

Cotton rose and said, "Now, now, ladies, let's not get into name-calling and hair-pulling. Let's hear the whole story first. Please sit down, Helen. You too, Miss Aldro. No harm in sitting down, is there? I think you both might like to hear more before you come to grips. As a lawyer, I'd like to hear the whole case before I decide anything. How about it?"

He made a big show of holding Nancy's chair for her. She sat down.

I jumped to hold Helen's chair. When it nudged the backs of her knees, she tried stubbornly to stay on her feet. With one hand and my knee maintaining forward pressure on the chair, I put the other hand on her shoulder. Against my strength and the leverage I could bring to bear, she had no chance. I outweighed her by about a hundred pounds of muscle and bone. She folded into the chair without a real struggle. Still, she was a strong woman, and I felt relieved she didn't decide to make a fight of it. I walked back to my seat, feeling her eyes scorching the back of my coat.

Aldro spoke, the clear mode of command ringing in his voice. An undertone of anger emphasized the formality of his words. "I don't know what the excitement is about. I came down here this evening expecting to meet a lawyer. I thought we'd just look each other over tonight and talk business tomorrow, but the marshal brought up the issue."

He shifted the sling supporting his wounded arm in a movement almost becoming habitual with him, seeking a more comfortable position.

"I need to consult a competent lawyer about what's been happening here, what I think may be behind it, and how I think I might need legal assistance. The facts are that two Dorcas brothers killed one of my men, wounded me, and tried to kill my daughter."

Aldro's hard gaze centered on Helen. "Judge Baynes killed those two men to save my daughter's life, probably saving her from dying in a particularly ugly way."

Then his stony face turned to Cotton, and his voice took an edge just short of open contempt. "If facts of this nature upset your sister so much, Mr. Sands, I question your judgment in bringing her with you and risking her exposure to such matters. I sent all the way to New York to obtain your services because Judge Baynes recommended you. I have great respect for his opinion."

No one moved or said a word. Helen blushed deeply, whether from embarrassment or anger I couldn't tell. His tone more sedate, Aldro said, "I suggest we speak of other matters, have a meal, and discuss business tomorrow."

We all sat stiffly in our chairs like scolded children. Aldro spoke once more. This time his tone came out apologetic. "You must forgive us, Miss Sands. We sometimes forget that our ways differ from those of New York. I'm from Texas, but I've taken quickly to Wyoming customs. In New York, women retire when the men discuss difficult and important subjects. In Wyoming, the women are expected to stay and help. Unlike the rest of the country, Wyoming women even vote and serve on juries. My daughter may have misread your desire to withdraw. She may have thought you indifferent to our problems."

Aldro's gaze shifted, and I looked up to see Bobby Nels standing in the door, holding a package. Aldro said, "Did you find what you wanted, son?"

"Yes, sir."

Aldro said quietly, "This is Bobby Nels, brother to the fine man who was killed doing honest work for me. Mr. Nels, this is Mr. Roland Sands, and this is Miss Helen Sands."

Bobby stepped forward to shake hands with Cotton. Then he turned to Helen, bowed, and said smoothly, "Enchanted, ma'am." Little Lord Fauntleroy couldn't have done it any better. I threw a surprised glance toward Aldro, and he allowed a trace of a smile to show.

Bobby turned to me. "Judge, I figured a simple thank you for all you did for me and my brother wasn't enough. There's no way to pay a man back for such a kindness, but I want you to have a little token of my gratitude. I want to give you this, sir." He extended the package toward me.

I stood to receive it. "Bobby, you didn't need to do anything like this."

He smiled up at me and said, "Go ahead and open it, Judge."

The outer paper fell away to reveal a sturdy black box. Inside, wrapped in a layer of delicate tissue and bound in a thick cowhide cover, lay a copy of the Book.

Bobby said, "I saw yours was awful worn, Judge. You had a hard time keeping the pages from flying away in the wind when you read for Larry. It was the only gift I could think of that I was sure you'd take. A man can't refuse the Book, can he?"

Something about it went straight through me. Maybe the idea of this young fellow thinking of a kindhearted gift for me in the middle of his grief tore me up. Maybe sheer surprise had something to do with it. Anyhow, something inside me buckled at the sight of this boy, dressed almost in rags, proudly handing over an obviously expensive gift, his face bright with hope his offering would bring pleasure.

Tears burst from my eyes. Young Nels saw my difficulty, and he tried to cover me by standing between me and the others, but he was too short. I couldn't figure how to hide the embarrassing flood, so I turned my face away from those seated at the table. If I so much as reached for my handkerchief, they'd know. Bobby shifted his feet, moving around me to try to make it look natural, as if I had turned to face him.

I knew my voice wouldn't work, so I whispered, "You got it right, Bobby. Nobody can refuse this kind of gift."

"I tried to get one exactly the same size as your old one, near as I could tell. I know you always carry it. This should fit your pocket too, just like the old one."

I wondered if the boy kept talking just to give me a chance to get myself put back together. The smooth leather cover seemed to caress my hand. "I never saw a Bible a man would be more proud to carry."

"I sure hope you like it. Could I ask a favor, Judge?"

"Anything."

"Could I have the one you used when you read for Larry? I'd like to have it, if you'd be willing to part with it."

I pulled it from my coat pocket and handed it to him. "You have to hold it just right, like this, or the pages fall out."

"Yes, sir. I saw how you held it before. A Book like this comes to be part of the man who carries it. I'll hear you saying good words for Larry every time I touch it."

Someone gripped my arm. Blinking like a fool I saw Cotton's blurred figure beside me. He held Helen's arm with his other hand.

Cotton said, "This is the man so mean he frightened you."

She took my hand with one of hers and reached up with the other to dab at my face with a perfumed handkerchief. "Doesn't matter. I fell in love with him anyway."

TWENTY

ALDRO MUST HAVE GIVEN the cook a signal, because he started bringing in steaming platters. Young Nels had already had his supper, so he excused himself and went to bed. I guess everybody was hungry, because conversation lagged while we ate. After the meal, Aldro's eyelids began to droop, and he said good night.

Marshal Lorimer stood around looking uncomfortable until I couldn't stand it. His relieved grin lighted the room when I told him to consider himself my guest for the meal.

As soon as he left, I turned to Nancy and asked, "When do I get my Navy back?"

Helen asked, "Navy?"

Nancy gave her an amused glance. "It's a revolver. Mr. Colt, a famous gun maker, sold many of them to the U.S. Navy."

"You borrowed a revolver from Luke?"

"Yes, and he's been whining to get it back ever since."

"What in the world would you want with a revolver?"

Nancy rubbed her mouth with a tiny hand, gave me one of her childlike looks, and made a show of considering her answer. Her gaze drifted back to Helen, and she said softly, "I cut my teeth on a loaded revolver. They make wonderful pacifiers. I like to suck on one when I'm nervous."

Cotton broke into a coughing spasm and fumbled for his napkin.

I said mildly, "Did you learn to talk like that in school back east?"

Nancy smiled at me. "Graduated at the top of my class. They wanted me to stay and be an instructor. You know that."

"You seem to know quite a bit about Miss Aldro, Luke," Helen said in a blandly dangerous voice. "Have you known her long?"

Nancy spoke before I could open my mouth. "You get to know a man quickly when you spend the night with him. Did you know he has terrible nightmares, Miss Sands?"

Helen blushed so deeply her eyes watered, but she never wavered. "No, I didn't. I've never spent the night with him."

"He's a kind man, and it tortures him to hurt people, but he's tough, and he does what he must. He never flinches from his duty. Did you know that, Miss Sands?" Nancy made each question directed at Helen into a barb, a thinly veiled insult.

"Perhaps not as well as you seem to, Miss Aldro."

"When I came here on the train, my daddy lay wounded out in the country. Nobody came to meet me. Luke gave me his room and wandered off into the night. I don't know where he finally found a place to rest. He paid for my meals. He bought me that coat you admired and hired a wagon to take me home through a blizzard. Did you know he feels a responsibility to help people in distress, Miss Sands?"

Helen sent a speculative look in my direction. "No. How kind of him."

I tried to lighten the crackling tension. "Only pretty girls in distress. Very pretty ones."

Both women gave me a hard glance, like my mama used to do when I belched at the table.

Nancy went on as if she hadn't heard me. "Luke saw those two men who tried to kill us while they were still far off. He suspected they were dangerous and warned me, but he kept going straight ahead. It never crossed his mind to try to run away. He loaned me one of his guns. I killed one of those men, Miss Sands, because Luke waited too long, wanted to be too sure. Luke killed the other one. Then he had nightmares because he hates killing so much. Did you know that, Miss Sands?"

"No. How could I?"

"Luke told me he fell in love with a New York woman who only saw his bad points. Aren't you that woman, Miss Sands?"

Helen hesitated briefly before she answered. "Yes."

"I don't know what bad points you thought you saw, Miss Sands. Luke is my friend. He saved my life. He buried one of my father's most trusted hired men with extraordinary concern. You saw how the man's brother felt about it. Luke helped care for my wounded father. Did you know that, Miss Sands?"

"No." Helen glanced at me. "I've hardly had a chance to talk to him since I came here."

"I never saw such pain on a man's face as when I woke him that night we spent together. We took turns with Bobby Nels, standing guard over my father and keeping the fire going. I watched Luke when he thought I was asleep. Did you know you caused pain, Miss Sands?"

"To myself, yes, I knew I caused terrible pain. To him, I didn't know how much."

"If you cause him any more misery, Miss Sands, I'll make

you eat that Colt revolver I borrowed from Luke. Can you understand that, Miss Sands?"

"Yes. I think I do understand now. In fact, I think I realized just this moment why you're talking to me like this. I'm not the threat you think me to be. I see no reason we can't be friends, Miss Aldro. I look forward to the chance to prove that."

Helen stretched out a hand, and Nancy stared at it for a long time before she took it.

Nancy said, "Luke has a blood feud to face. You heard the marshal. Do you know what that means, Miss Sands?"

"For heaven's sake, call me Helen. Yes, I think I know what that means."

"Wouldn't it be tragic if Luke was slow to defend himself because he worried about what you'd think?"

Helen turned to face me. "That would be a false worry."

I cocked an eye at Cotton. "See what happens when the men let women discuss important and difficult matters in Wyoming? The men can't get a word in edgewise."

Cotton, who had listened in wide-eyed silence after his coughing spell, leaned forward intently and said, "Any woman that loyal to her friends would make a superb wife. Miss Aldro, will you marry me?"

She turned on him, eyelids drooping in what she probably figured was her seductive look. "My daddy's probably going to spend all his money on an expensive lawyer. I want a big wedding. We'll have to wait until after he markets his cattle next summer."

Cotton turned to Helen and me. "My God, that sounded like she said yes. Now I'm the Sands that's frightened."

Helen smiled at her brother. "Serves you right, you and your risqué jokes." She still held Nancy's hand.

Nancy said, "Judge Luke Baynes heard you propose, Mr. Sands. If you trifle with my affections, he'll put you in jail if he doesn't shoot you. What do you call the charge in court when a man trifles with a lady's affections, Judge Baynes?" Nancy still held a straight face.

"Idiocy, my lady. Aggravated idiocy if the woman grew up with a loaded Colt pacifier."

Helen burst into laughter, and the rest of us joined her. Cotton had timed his little joke perfectly, and Nancy turned the tables on him adroitly. All of us needed to take a deep breath and enjoy a good laugh. The cook came out of the kitchen wearing his coat. We took the signal and went upstairs to bed.

ALDRO HAD A TABLE and another chair carried up to his room. He and Cotton spent the next morning with their heads together while I presided over my court. We met in the hotel dining room for lunch.

After the others finished the noon meal, they made a point of going about their business, leaving Helen and me at the table. As soon as we sat alone in the empty dining room, she put her hand on my wrist.

"I won't be going back to New York with Cotton."

"Oh?"

"A man I love asked me to come to Wyoming. I'm a few days late, but I'm here."

"Why did the man you love ask you to come out here?"

"I stopped him before he could tell me. Now I've got to get him started again."

"He was going to ask you to marry him."

"I accept."

"I didn't ask. I just said I was going to."

"Ask then."

"Can't. You scared me off. You're like two women. One has a wonderful mind and is kind and sweet. The other one is a ninny who terrifies me."

She laughed, a wonderful, bubbling sound. "How do you suppose Mean Luke and Ninny Helen will get along?"

"Hard to tell."

"Luke, I've been through hell finding out that I love you so much. I nearly died when you left." Her vulnerability to blushing began to show again. "You won't ask me to marry you, will you?"

"I started to do that once and you shot me through both of my over-large feet, a terrifying and painful experience."

"Then I'll have to ask you. Luke, will you marry me?"

I looked down at the scars on my knuckles and spoke in my measured, judicial voice. "That's a question upon which a man must cerebrate carefully. Impetuous adjudication can precipitate adverse consequences which cool prognostication could easily circumvent. A sophisticated man withdraws intuitively from a contract susceptible to emotional hazards inherent with an indecisive and unpredictable associate."

She leaned forward to interrupt me, but I raised a hand to stop her. She burst out, "I'm not indecisive and unpredictable anymore!"

I put on an impatient expression and closed my eyes as if I didn't want to hear another word. She settled back.

"Nonetheless, a positive response could possibly be justified in extreme circumstances when even a circumspect collaborator finds himself compelled by the press of rising temperature and a coercive suspicion that the opportunity is episodic and perforce might not recur."

"Luke, what on earth are you talking about?"

"I said yes." I leaned forward and kissed her. "Because you make me all hot and bothered and this kind of opportunity might not come again. I thought you liked lawyer talk."

"I thought you were going to say no."

"Why?"

"You've been distant ever since I came here."

"I'm learning to be urbane. Cotton's teaching me."

"There's nothing good you can learn from my brother. You

should be teaching him. You could at least try to be romantic."

"I did. I just kissed you in broad daylight in a room with big
windows leading to the street. I have to keep up appearances.
What would all my drunks think if they saw that? Want me to
be really romantic? I'll tap on your door tonight about midnight."

Her face took on color. "You will not. Cotton hears everything."

"How can I be romantic when my feeble advances get so
ruthlessly rebuffed? A timid man like me is easily crushed."

She said, "Unless . . ."

"Unless what?"

"Well, uh . . ."

"Unless we get married this afternoon? Yeah, that's right."

"You want to get married this afternoon, Luke?"

"I don't want to look too eager. I'm trying to be urbane."

"I'm not supposed to be eager either. It's not ladylike."

I sighed heavily. "With you being ladylike and me being
urbane, we'll probably never have any fun."

She showed signs of developing a permanent blush, but
she'd evidently made up her mind not to take a backward step.
I began to realize she'd done a lot of thinking before she left
New York. Helen Sands, if she'd had any doubts before, was
sending every kind of signal that she knew her own mind now.

She studied the tablecloth in front of her. "Is midnight the
best time to have fun?"

"Anytime is the best time to have fun. All you have to do is
stuff Cotton's ears with cotton."

"Why don't we get married this afternoon, Luke? I'm eager. We'll stuff Cotton's ears onto a train heading for New
York."

"Because I'd like to invite my family to come, if they can
make it. How about in a couple or three weeks, more or less,
so I can gather the Baynes clan?"

She looked away, and I knew she didn't have the nerve to meet my eye when she asked, "Are you urbane enough to wait for two or three weeks?"

"Are you ninny enough to insist on it?"

She tapped her fingers nervously on the table. "I'm not sure. I never felt like this before."

I said, "Let's go tell Cotton. Maybe he'll stuff his own ears if I ask him to."

She sucked in a startled breath. "Luke, don't you dare. I'll die from embarrassment." She covered her face with her hands. "I'll turn into a puddle. You'll have to mop me up to bury me."

We made it to the landing where the stairs curved back. She stopped, looked up and down to be sure nobody was in sight. Then she pulled my head down and kissed me. I pretended to be wobbly-legged the rest of the way up. Surely the most joyful sound in the world is that of a happy woman laughing.

We tapped on Cotton's door and listened to him fumbling around getting into his coat. When he opened the door, I walked in and said urgently, "Cotton, I'm going to need all the money you have."

He glanced at Helen and asked, "Money? You need money?"

"I've accepted your sister's proposal of marriage. She swept me off my feet. We need to talk about wedding dresses, dowry, and all that stuff. Since you're the head of her family, you got to pay for all that."

He whooped, grabbed my hand, and pounded me with his free hand. Then he grabbed Helen and swung her round and round. "Great! I knew it would happen. Wonderful."

He stopped abruptly and stared at me. "I just realized what you said. You're right. This is going to cost me. How about half the entire Sands fortune? That sound generous enough? Well, never mind, this is no time to be petty."

He dug into his pocket and threw two bills on his bed.

"That'll be one dollar for you and one for me. If you'd waited until after I paid for supper tonight, the Sands fortune would have been completely depleted. I need to borrow money from you to buy a ticket to get back to New York."

Helen smiled at me. "I come with two carpetbags full of clothing. My wedding dress is ready. I have a lovely sable stole, although it has a little singed place on it. And I have four dollars."

I scooped up his two dollars and handed them to him. "I guess you can pay the debt over time, if we can agree on a rate of interest."

The Baynes clan had spread far and wide, and I admit to a feeling of impatience that day. Fact is, I didn't feel the least bit urbane. If my folks wanted to see me get married, they'd better hustle their hocks. I went down to the telegraph office that very afternoon.

Helen did too, only a few minutes behind me, but I didn't find out about that until much later.

TWENTY-ONE

COTTON WROTE FROM NEW YORK that he'd investigated, found the development company that was selling railroad land, and determined that they were, indeed, selling property already bought by Aldro and his Texas friends, plus large chunks of public domain. He applied for and obtained an injunction in New York against further sales, froze the assets of the company, and thought he might get part of the money back for those who had bought false titles.

Fraud charges were pending against the ringleaders, but

Cotton said he thought a payoff had been made. All the ac-
cused had vanished after posting a ridiculously small bail.

Cotton said some of his shadowy friends had slipped warnings to him, had picked up rumors that he'd made powerful
enemies who wanted revenge. He didn't take such tips lightly,
thought he'd been followed a couple of times, admitted being
edgy and cautious, and advised me to take precautions too. He
said a tall man like me had a broad back that made a tempting
target.

He also mentioned that he had decided to come to Wyoming and start into independent practice, because he'd never
have such a sweet opportunity elsewhere with a brother-in-
law on the bench. At the last, he said he hoped Nancy and her
daddy remained in Wyoming, because he looked forward to
their company.

Nancy wanted to stay in Cheyenne with Helen and be in
the wedding. She also made it plain that she wanted to be in
Wyoming when Cotton came back. Aldro wanted Nancy to
go home with him. They had a huge argument. Actually, Aldro argued and Nancy ignored him until he wore out. Aldro
and Bobby Nels went home to Texas a few days later. Nancy
stayed.

My routine settled into a happy rut. Helen loved the courtroom. Every morning, she'd come with me and sit quietly
through the proceedings. After court, Helen and I rode every
afternoon, cold weather or not. She had never been on a horse
before, and I had a grand time teaching her to ride. She
picked out a sweet-tempered mare as if she'd been judging
horses all her life. In spite of all my warnings, she let her
enthusiasm show. The hostler got his revenge on me, charged
two prices for that mare. What could I do, with her standing
there like a kid about to get her first pony?

In two days she'd made a pet of her horse, knew how to put
on the sidesaddle, and could mount unassisted if need be. After our ride, she'd jump into the cases on my trial docket,

arguing both sides with me if the case held anything beyond dull routine.

We sketched out a little house she thought we could afford and made plans to start building in the spring. She never took me seriously when I mentioned about a hundred times that money presented no serious limitation. It became obvious that Helen had never been in a situation where money wasn't a primary concern. That was fine with me. As long as a man's wife had that attitude, watchful and thrifty, money would probably never become a point of contention.

My family answered my telegrams, but they all had business they couldn't avoid on such short notice, so Helen and I went ahead and scheduled our marriage. Three days before the date we had set, Cotton came back to Cheyenne. Nancy, Helen, and I met him at the train station. When we got back to the hotel, he hardly touched his dinner.

At the end of the meal he spoke curtly, "Will you ladies please excuse us? I must talk to Luke in private." I think they were both too surprised to argue. They glanced at each other with wide eyes, rose, and went upstairs.

Cotton said, "Luke, a lot has happened since I wrote to you. I left New York in a blazing hurry. I hopped on the first train I could catch."

"What's going on?"

"When I went to Chance Lorane to give notice, to tell him I wanted to come out to Wyoming to practice, he beat me to the punch. Before I could say a word, he gave me a choice. Either I drop the case against the land development company or leave his firm."

"Is he representing them? Is there a conflict of interest?"

"No, Luke. I can't prove it and neither can Chance, but we've both got our sources of information. Pell Solder is behind the whole scheme. Chance says that Solder has his entire fortune tied up in this deal. The whole thing smells of Solder's method of operation. Chance is convinced that Solder hired the Dorcas family. While we were talking he changed his mind, said it was too late to try to withdraw gracefully. He dismissed me from the firm, said he didn't want to feel responsible for my death, and advised me to get out of New York as fast as possible."

"So what? You were going to come out here anyway."

"I have my sources of information too. I had friends whisper in my ear that money had been offered to get me killed. Not killed if I stayed in New York, Luke. Not killed unless I dropped the case. Killed, period."

"Sounds grim."

"There's more. Chance told me why he recommended you for a position on the bench out here. He said that was his way to get rid of you gracefully, said you were 'too ethically inflexible' for his kind of practice. He wasn't surprised when I told him my sources said that a judge out in Wyoming has got to go too."

"Me?"

"Who the hell else?"

"Why me?"

"Solder lost his ass on this deal. He's ruined, and he's hell-bent on revenge. He thinks you're Aldro's hired man. Why should he think that, Luke?"

I didn't dodge. I laid it out for him, told the story from start to finish. I ended with: "Aldro wanted a tough judge sympathetic to cattlemen. His money, and that of some other Texans just like him, put me on the bench."

Cotton leaned back in his chair and threw up his hands. "You lucky devil. Why didn't they ask me? I could grow fond of cattlemen if they'd put me on the bench."

"Yeah, but you're naturally corrupt. I'm honest. Aldro didn't want a dishonest judge, just a tough one."

"Don't try to joke about it, Luke. Both of us are in danger, honest or corrupt. After that train ride, I feel like I haven't slept for a week. Watch your back. I couldn't go to court with any of this. My sources don't testify in courts. They either vanish or suffer loss of memory. But it's the truth. I know it as sure as I'm sitting here."

I put a hand on his shoulder. "I came out here to simplify my life, Cotton. I fell in love with a New York lady, but she ran me off. Then she changed her mind and followed me out here. Her brother is my best friend, but he stirred up enemies who want to kill me. My life seems to get simpler by the day."

JEDEDIAH JACOBSON, the newspaperman, came to see me at noon the next day in the hotel dining room. Helen, Cotton, Nancy, and I looked up when Jacobson dropped a poster on the dinner table in front of me.

Jacobson said, "They'll be by this afternoon to pick those up. I printed fifty of them."

The poster read:

**NO MAN KILLS A DORCAS WITHOUT
ANSWERING FOR IT.
JUSTICE DEMANDS
AN EYE FOR AN EYE AND A TOOTH
FOR A TOOTH.
JETHRO DORCAS**

Cotton sprang to his feet and stood beside the wall, scanning the street through one of the dining room windows. "Have you seen them, Rube? Do you know what they look like?"

"No, but Marshal Lorimer said they were alike as peas in a pod. The two I shot were tall, beefy men with a shock of shaggy black hair. They wore beards and dressed like mountain men, all in leather and furs."

"Would you run upstairs to my room, Helen? Look in my brown bag. Please bring my big revolver down to me." Cotton flicked a glance at me and said apologetically, "I'm only carrying my two derringers you gave me. I'd like to have my target pistol."

Helen rose and headed for the stairs without another word. When she returned and handed the pistol, holster, and belt to him, he said, "Sit down by Luke over there away from the windows."

The hotel clerk looked in. "What's going on, got trouble?"

Jacobson showed him the poster and asked, "What made you suspect there might be trouble?"

"I don't have women trotting through my lobby toting guns every day. Want me to send the cook for the marshal, Judge?"

"I'd be obliged. Maybe he can head off trouble."

He walked quickly to the kitchen, and I heard the back door slam shut before he came back. He spoke as he crossed the dining room toward the lobby. "Cookie left so fast the air in the kitchen smells like burnt feathers. I better get back to my desk."

Cotton said, "These walls won't stop rifle slugs, Rube." He tilted a table on its side, pushed it against the wall, and knelt behind it. "Nancy, you and Helen would be better off upstairs until we see what's going to happen down here."

Helen looked at me, and I nodded agreement. She rose at once and went to the lobby door.

Nancy said, "I can't help if I'm up there. I'm staying."

Cotton said mildly, "If you give me any backchat, I'll stuff you in a corner and pile tables on you till I feel you're safe."

She stared at his back for a long count of about ten. He ignored her. Finally, she came to her feet and marched out behind Helen. Cotton aimed a smug grin at me.

I said, "The tone of voice sounded fine, but the words you selected for your closing argument seemed a bit primitive."

"Don't lecture me on how to persuade women, especially

that one. She knew for dead certain I'd do exactly what I said. Sincerity, Rube, gives a man a golden tongue."

"You see anything out there?"

"I see a bunch of people who don't look the least bit like dark men in leather and furs." He glanced back at Jacobson. "I see an idiot in a good place to get his butt shot off."

Jacobson said, "That's correct. My goodness, I must find a better vantage point." He moved two tables into position in a corner, pushed them onto their sides, and sat down in a chair behind his little barricade.

"Why don't you get out of here?" I asked.

"An assassination attempt against a territorial judge and a lawyer is front-page news. I need to be here."

Cotton asked, "Born that way, do you suppose? Or maybe his mama dropped him on his head."

"There must be something coarsening about the legal system," Jacobson said. "Law enforcement officers, lawyers, and judges all seem predisposed to gratuitous invective and crude deportment."

"Here comes the marshal," Cotton announced. "At the rate he's walking, he may not be here before dark."

Moments later, Lorimer walked in with the cook on his heels. "How about coffee? Got any fresh coffee?" The cook trotted toward his kitchen.

Lorimer glanced at the upended tables and asked, "You boys getting ready for a big war?"

I said, "Look at that poster Jacobson is waving at you."

He stared at the poster. His finger stopped under each word as he read with agonizing slowness. "Nice job, wouldn't you say? Got all the words spelled right, I think."

Cotton's eyes met mine. I asked, "You smell something?"

"I think so."

Lorimer pulled a large envelope from under his vest and dropped it on a table. "Have a seat and read this, Judge."

The message inside was brief and simple. It read:

Judge Luke Baynes,
This crosses one item off my list.
Yr. Obt. Svt.,
Baxter Aldro, Texan

Inside, folded neatly, was a copy of Jacobson's poster.

I turned to Cotton. "Relax. Forget watching the street. Come over here and look at this."

Cotton crossed the room and read the note. "What list?"

"I got off a few remarks about crazy Texans and whatnot. Also, I might have pulled a little joke or two on him here and there. He said he was keeping a list he planned to make me work off as soon as he got well."

Cotton made a pained face. "You pulled a little joke or two, did you? Like what? Like shooting his cattle? He's got a tough sense of humor. Of course, he doesn't know what we're really up against."

Jacobson, ever the curious reporter, asked with sadistic pleasure, "How many items does Mr. Aldro have on that list?"

TWENTY-TWO

ALDRO'S JOKE may have saved Cotton's life.

When we walked out the door of the hotel, he'd hardly taken two steps onto the front porch before he gave a surprised grunt like he'd been hit in the belly and sprang to his left. Fast moves like that had long meant danger in my life. He moved so quickly, my trail reflexes took command. Without thinking, I jumped in the opposite direction just as a rifle cracked. The bullet tugged at my sleeve as I dropped away from the doorway. The wicked, booming smack from inside told me that the shot passed through the doorway and probably struck the solid oak hotel desk in the lobby behind me.

The heavy cloud of powder smoke drifting from an alley across the street said "buffalo gun" as clearly as a signature in the air. Navy in hand, I could see no target. The street had emptied like magic. A quick glance found Cotton on one knee, just now drawing his revolver and swinging his head tensely from side to side, trying to find the shooter.

"I saw him just in time, Rube. Didn't even have time to warn you. Are you hit?"

"No. Got a hole through the sleeve of a thirty-five-dollar coat."

"I don't see him now. He must have beat it down that alley. Think he'll try again?"

"Probably not. From the sound and the smoke, I think he fired a big Sharps. He can't reload that thing very fast."

Lorimer's voice came from the doorway. "What happened? Who shot?"

Cotton might as well have been reviewing the facts for a jury. "I happened to look right at him when I came through the door, or I'd be a dead man now. Lucky. And Luke's still alive because he's quick as a scared frog. A man was raising his rifle when he stepped out of the alley. Must have been waiting for us to come out the door. I took one look, knew he was a Dorcas, and jumped for the floor. Good thing we'd been talking about what they look like only a minute ago."

I said, "I'm going across the street. Cover me while I take a look. Lorimer says they come in bunches, so there may be more than one after us."

"Be careful, Rube."

"You too, Cotton. You owe me money."

His chuckle followed me as I raced across the road to the front of the general store and edged along the front of it. The owner and his customers stared round-eyed at me from behind counters and merchandise displays. One of the customers looked vaguely familiar, but I had more to do than puzzle about that. The alley lay empty. I waved at Cotton, and he charged across the street with Lorimer on his heels.

"I'm going after him. Watch my back."

Without waiting for an answer, I started picking my way through garbage, moving through a narrow space hardly wider than my shoulders between the two buildings. Before I got halfway to the end, I heard horses kicked to a gallop. I ran the rest of the way, but by the time I reached the back, the area behind the buildings stood deserted as a ghost town.

Cotton stood facing the street at the other end of the alley. At my wave he trotted to me. Lorimer, six-gun in hand, took a slow look around the street before he followed.

"I think I heard them leave. Sounded like two horses. Don't let somebody shoot me while I try to find tracks."

Cotton nodded.

I took my time. Probably the most nerve-wracking thing a man can do is to puzzle out a trail when somebody may be lining sights on him. I had to force myself to walk with all my attention focused on the ground, looking for fresh, deep marks among the hundreds of boot tracks and hoof prints. Grown men almost never run in town, nor do they kick their horses into a wild gallop, so I felt sure I could find traces in the packed snow. Sure enough, I found prints. Surprisingly, the two horses were unshod. Cotton followed a step behind me, gun in hand, head swinging like an owl, while I tracked the two animals to the edge of town. Lorimer trailed farther behind, watching our backs.

When I straightened and took a deep breath, Cotton asked, "You think you found their trail? Can you be sure among all these tracks?"

"Positive, no. Sure, yes. I'm sure enough that if I catch up with them, I won't hesitate to burn powder."

"You plan to go after them?"

"I do. It's a Baynes family trait, Cotton."

"What? What're you talking about?"

I turned away from the trail of two unshod horses and spun the cylinder of my Navy so I could lower the hammer on the empty cylinder. "The Baynes clan sleeps peacefully, Cotton, because we bury people who shoot at us. We find that restful." The Navy dropped gently into my holster.

"Damn, Cotton, I just thought of something else. I saw a man in the store when I ran across the street. It just clicked in my mind who he might be. I think it was Pell Solder. I wish I'd paid more attention to him in Morrissey's carriage."

"You saw him here in Cheyenne?"

I struck out into a swift walk back toward the store. "I'm going to see if he's still around."

"Hold on there, boys. Where you headed so fast, and what kind of trail you been following, Judge?" Lorimer closed the gap he'd held, guarding our backs.

I answered, "Two unshod ponies. I think I can follow them if I can get on the trail quick."

"Show me the tracks."

Cotton said, "I'll go look for our man, Rube. You show Lorimer what you've been following. I wouldn't know one track from another." He walked off toward the store, giving me no chance to argue.

Lorimer's brows went up. "Look for our man? What man? You think another one is still in town?"

"Come on." I turned back toward the spot where we'd left the trail. It took only a few moments to show the marshal a couple of fairly clear places where the prints were plain. As I expected, he squatted down several times and examined the tracks from several angles. When he came to his feet, I'd bet Lorimer would recognize those tracks anywhere.

"You stick to your judging. I'll do the trailing. This is marshal work. You already did enough marshaling when you shot those two boys and started all this."

"You can deputize me if you want, but I'm going after

them, Lorimer. Look at this new coat." I showed him the hole in my sleeve. "This coat cost me thirty-five dollars."

He blanched. "What did they do, sew gold dust in the lining? I didn't know they made coats that cost that much. Never mind. You stay in town, get yourself married, and act like a judge. I'll get up a posse and act like a marshal. I know where they live anyway. I should have gone out and talked to old man Dorcas before this got out of hand."

"Talk?"

"Yeah. It's worth a try. Might have a chance to make a little peace parlay. Never can tell."

As we walked back toward the hotel, I found myself in a quandary. The Baynes clan always handled our own trouble, but as a judge I felt trapped. Maybe Lorimer had it right. Maybe it showed better sense for me to sit tight and let the law handle this. For certain, I didn't look forward to telling Helen that we'd get married later, just as soon as I got back from shooting a few more people.

"All right, Marshal. You try to settle this peacefully if you can."

"Good. I'll be leaving in an hour." He turned away to head toward the stable.

When I walked up the steps to the hotel porch, I waved at Helen and Nancy, who stood framed in the front window. As soon as I closed the door, Nancy asked, "Where's Cotton?"

"I saw a man from New York in the store. Seeing him out here made us curious. Cotton went looking for him. Now, I guess I'd better go look for Cotton."

Helen asked, "What happened to the man who shot at you?"

I'd fallen into the habit of fingering the hole in my sleeve. Her question reminded me of it, and I jerked my hand away too quick. The move drew her attention.

"I think there were two of them. They got away. Lorimer plans to gather a posse and try to trail them down."

She grabbed the sleeve and examined the holes, front and back. "This is a bullet hole, isn't it?"

"Moths are bad out here, even in the winter."

Nancy helped me with a solemn, "They don't come any closer than that, do they, Luke? Did you know the slug went through the desk and nicked the hotel clerk's leg? Just a crease and a few splinters, but he turned bed-wetting pale. He must've bled ten drops. He danced in a circle on one foot for quite awhile. Surprised me. Pretty good dancer for a town man."

I shouldn't have grinned, but I couldn't help it. "You're a sympathetic little twitter box."

Helen said quietly, "I don't see anything funny. What's wrong with me? Everybody seems to be having a good time but me."

"Where'd Jacobson, my favorite newspaperman, go?"

Nancy said, "He was in the corner behind two tables when I came downstairs. He popped up, saw your Navy in my hand, and dove back out of sight. Did you see him leave, Helen? He may still be hiding in the dining room."

Jacobson spoke from the dining room doorway. "I'm not hiding, Miss Aldro. That's a most unkind thing to say. I'm maintaining the best vantage point to get the news. What's all this about, Judge Baynes?"

"You'd best ask the marshal."

"Where is he?"

"Leaving with a posse. Maybe he'll let you go along."

"I don't ride well. After about an hour, I can dismount and empty a handful of skin out of my boots. I'll try to interview him before he leaves." He walked to the front door.

Before the door shut, Nancy said, "I'm sure the marshal will be glad to see you."

He flashed a tired smile over his shoulder and kept going.

"I'd better go find Cotton."

Nancy offered my second Navy. "Think you'll need this?"

"No. You look after it a little while longer."

I hadn't walked a hundred feet before Jed's wagon thundered down the street, team at a gallop. He pulled rein and yelled, "You better come quick, Judge. A couple of strangers got your little friend trapped down at Miss Deveroux's place."

My butt hit the seat before the wagon stopped, and Jed snapped the reins to put the team back to a gallop. He spat to the side and said, "Grabbed him from both sides. Big men. Never seen 'em before. Peeled his guns off and acted like they plan to beat him to death."

He brought the team sliding to a halt, and I hit the ground running. My Navy in hand and cocked, I pushed the door open so hard it crashed against the wall with a splintering crack. Cotton lay in the center of the barroom floor, face down. Rooster Delaney stood with his back to the bar grinning down at Cotton's still form. When the door burst open, Delaney swung toward me, raising Cotton's pistol. Rooster was born strong, but slow.

I shot him.

TWENTY-THREE

DELANEY STARED AT ME, blinking stupidly.

"Put the gun down, Rooster."

He nodded and placed the pistol gently on the bar. With his eyes still on me, he asked, "Why'd you shoot me?"

"In this part of the country, you don't turn toward a man and lift a gun. It's unfriendly, Rooster."

He nodded again, lifted a hand to his chest, and said, "My mistake. Shouldn't have left New York. Don't know nothing about guns anyhow. Funny, it don't hurt much. Seems like it ought to hurt like hell."

My Navy moving back and forth, I checked the other men in the bar. Everyone had his eyes on Rooster. Close beside Cotton's prostrate form sat Sailor O'Dell, a sardonic grin on his face. Blood stained the knuckles of both hands on the table in front of him.

"You been beating on that little fellow, Rooster?"

"Naw, I just helped hold him and take his guns away. Sailor done the beating."

"Why?"

"Money. Guy named Pell Solder paid us to do it. Pell came out all the way from New York with us. Wanted to be sure we got the job done."

Delaney's gaze slowly swung across the room.

"He was here just a minute ago. Wonder where he went. Where's Pell, Sailor?"

O'Dell said, "He ducked out, Rooster. Went out the back door when this fellow busted his way in."

Delaney's attention seemed to wander back to me. "We was supposed to get you too, Fifi." His lean on the bar grew heavier, and his trousers couldn't hide the trembling of his legs.

"Bartender, give him a drink. You want to sit down, Rooster?"

The bartender sprang forward with a bottle and filled the glass beside Cotton's pistol.

Delaney, blood now coursing freely between the fingers of his left hand against his chest, picked up the glass with his right. He lifted it toward me and tossed down the whiskey.

"Thanks, Fifi. I'm fine."

He dropped his bloody left hand to the bar, but it wouldn't hold him. Gently he slid down until he sat on the floor, the crimson hand still clutching the edge of the bar. The room remained perfectly quiet as his grim hold gradually relaxed.

Rooster looked up at me with a smirk. "Fooled you, didn't I, Fifi? I lied, and you swallowed it. I tried my best to shoot you. Actually, I'm pretty good with a gun. You were always too quick for me, just too damn quick."

When his grip failed at last, Rooster settled gently to his side, cheek resting on the sawdust, eyes fixed. Only then did the shot glass roll from his hand, making a slow circle on the floor beside him before it came to rest. When his thick form fell away from the bar, I saw the two derringers I'd given Cotton lying close to his pistol.

LaRue Deveroux stepped forward and bent over Cotton. Sailor said harshly, "Don't touch him."

She ignored him and started to roll Cotton over. Without rising, O'Dell lashed out, struck her a wicked backhand to the cheek, dumping her on the floor beside Cotton. Every other man in the room surged to his feet.

I swung the Navy in slow back-and-forth arcs. "Easy, men. Everybody just sit back down nice and slow."

O'Dell sneered. "Big talk behind a big gun. You ever put that thing down and act like a man?"

"Jed?"

"Yeah, Judge?"

"You know how to shoot a Navy?"

"Passable well, Judge. I ain't a stranger to it."

"Can you handle this one good enough to keep anybody from bothering me?"

"Guaranteed, Judge. Good as money in the bank."

I handed the Navy to him and stripped off my coat. O'Dell's eyes widened in surprise, and a big grin appeared.

LaRue came to her feet, lithe as a cat, and walked behind the bar. She stepped on something, perhaps a box, because she swung herself up effortlessly and walked down the top of the bar until she came to Cotton's guns. She sat down, dangled her legs off the edge over Rooster's body, arranged a derringer carefully beside each thigh, and picked up Cotton's pistol.

Using both thumbs to cock it, she held it in both hands between her knees. Then she glanced at me and said, "If Jed needs help, I'm ready now, Judge." A single drop of blood slid from her nose down her upper lip. She didn't bother to wipe it away.

Cotton rolled over and sat up, his face a bloody mess.

"You hear me, Cotton?"

"Yeah, Rube."

"Can you get up?"

"Let's see." He came carefully to his feet, using a chair to steady himself, knees quaking.

"Go sit on the bar with the lady, Cotton. Can you do that?"

LaRue snapped to the bartender, "Go help him."

O'Dell sprang to his feet and pointed his finger at the bartender. "Don't try it. Don't move."

That's when I hit him a beaut, a sucker punch, as pretty a surprise right cross as I ever threw, right on the button. O'Dell had finally given me the opening I wanted, shifted his eyes from me for a critical split second. The pleasant shock of a solid blow vibrated up my arm clear to the shoulder. O'Dell, caught by a punch he never saw coming, hit the sawdust shoulders first.

Sir John Sholto Douglas, 8th Marquis and Earl of Queensberry, who published his fine rules for boxers in 1867, would have been appalled. I pulled off my string tie and laughed.

The bartender rushed forward, threw an arm around Cotton, and hurried him behind the bar.

O'Dell lay flat on his back for a count of six or eight, but the sound of my laughter seemed to snap him awake. He jerked his head off the floor, blinked in comical surprise, and rolled to his feet. As he straightened, I tried to lift him to the ceiling with a sweeping hook to the ribs. His explosive gasp reminded me of Jeremy Pitts when he met the muzzle of my Navy. O'Dell went down again.

He spun on his hip, trying to leg-whip my feet from under

me. I hopped over his swinging leg and kicked him in the face when he sprawled off balance from the missed attempt. Again, the nice jolt of a solid blow vibrated up from my heel and caused me to laugh. O'Dell staggered up, his face twisted with rage and a broad stream of blood gushing from both nostrils. He crouched and circled, fists loosely doubled. I'd seen loose fists before, the mark of a fighter who liked to flick slack fingers at his opponent's eyes.

I grinned into his face and asked sympathetically, "Want to stop and wipe your nose?" The sound of scraping told me the men in the saloon were shoving tables back to give us room, but I kept my eyes on O'Dell.

Outside, somebody on the street shouted, "Fight! Fight!"

O'Dell flicked a left jab and moved away, weight nicely balanced on quick feet. His experience showed immediately. Now he was trying to feel me out, trying to discover what he was up against and start to work on flaws. His caution showed in that first jab. It fell short, and I didn't even bother to block it, just answered with one of my own. He slipped it neatly and responded instantly with a loose-fingered flick at my eyes. I grabbed at his hand and almost had it, but he jerked away, blinking in surprise again.

The fear of the loose-fisted fighter against an experienced opponent is that one of his blows will be caught in midair. If I succeeded in grabbing a couple of fingers, I'd break them like twigs, and he knew it. I gave O'Dell another grim smile when I saw his fists tighten. He'd decided that trick wasn't worth the risk of another attempt when I almost had him on the first try.

I feinted with a right lead. I figured he'd respond. Since I'd caught him with a sucker punch once and put him down, he'd respect the power in that wallop, and he'd expect me to try it again. He rolled his shoulders forward to slip under my right and threw his own. I sidestepped and caught him with a jab to the ear, and blood spread down his neck from a crushed earlobe before I could throw the next punch. My right cross went high when he began to bob and weave. Then he sprang in with a ripping left hook.

He caught me solidly on the cheek and lights flashed before my eyes. He stopped and stood like a fool, waiting for me to fall. My right to the cheek staggered him, and I heard a rumble of laughter from the watchers. He began to bob and weave under my jabs and caught me with a couple of wicked hooks to the body. Again, his expression told me he expected me to fold, showed the grim confidence of the power hitter, but hours on end at the business end of both pick and ax build a midsection that can take punishment. Still, I couldn't take much more of that. O'Dell qualified as the most dangerous body puncher I'd ever faced.

I circled, legs gone heavy the way they do when a man takes heavy body punishment, and caught him with two jabs, forcing him back. I rubbed the cheek, and a quick glance showed a plentiful smear of blood on the back of my hand. The ringing in my ears, a bulging cheek, and a telltale smudge of blood on my hand indicated the price. The information I paid the price for was that Sailor O'Dell's power lay in his left hook, and he could hit with the best. That meant he'd always try to move in close.

O'Dell had learned a couple of things too. I knew the game, and he couldn't expect to catch me with simple tricks. Also, he'd found out that Baynes men have heads like solid stone, and one punch wouldn't take me down.

O'Dell's breath came in sucking gasps now, and I feinted with a jab twice in quick succession. His eyes flickered and, for a moment, I saw desperation. He stepped back, but I followed and threw a right to the heart. His wicked hook whipped by my nose, an inch short, and I nailed him with another right to the cheek before he could recover. His knees buckled and I threw another right. Often the same blow thrown in quick succession, one after another, will work wonders. The last right dropped him. He lay on one hip and one elbow, staring emptily into space. He never saw it coming when I wound up and kicked him in the face again. The kick put him flat, one leg jerking convulsively.

I backed to the bar, taking deep breaths. My legs trembled under me as if I'd already gone twenty rounds. If we'd been in the ring, we'd have been given a rest between rounds to recover, but barroom brawls don't allow for such luxuries. My cheek felt tighter with each passing second, and I knew I didn't have long before I'd have trouble with the swelling. Fighting with one eye swollen shut is a harsh thing to face. O'Dell didn't move. I prayed he'd stay down.

"Water."

The bartender spun a pitcher down the bar to me. I rinsed my mouth and carefully spat bloody water into a nearby spittoon. The sting told me I had a split lip, but I didn't even remember catching a blow to the mouth. I glanced at LaRue and said, "I'm trying to be tidy." Her answering smirk showed clearly over the rim of the pitcher as I took a couple of swallows.

Freed from the fierce concentration I'd had to focus on Sailor, the babble of voices around me began to sink in.

Somebody said, "Damnedest fight I ever saw. Couple of damned giants. I bet both of 'em weigh 250 pounds."

Another said, "You just get here, Sam? You missed a good 'un. I been here through the whole thing. Two of 'em jumped on that little feller sitting on the bar beside LaRue. The judge shot one and pounded the other into pig slops."

When I looked around, the barroom had filled with men, was packed wall-to-wall. More stood outside the front windows and crowded the front and back doors. Both doors stood wide open and to hell with the cold.

O'Dell and I hadn't moved around much. The whole fight could have happened in a ten-foot ring. We hadn't broken a stick of furniture.

I asked, "You feeling better, Cotton?" My voice came out a bit awkward; my swelling lips didn't seem to fit together right.

"I feel like the Seventh Cavalry rode over my face. You all right, Rube?"

"Yeah, just fine." I touched my cheek. It felt like it had grown to the size of an orange. Blood dripped from my beard to a soaked shirtfront. A quick glance at the mirror behind the bar showed a streaming cut high on my cheekbone and an eye fast becoming a mere slit. After all the scuffling around I'd done in my life, I'd picked up my first serious cut. It'd make a fine scar.

O'Dell stirred and slowly came to his hands and knees, head hanging. One of the crowd said grimly, "That bastard hit LaRue, knocked her down, bloodied her nose. You through with him, Judge?"

Before I could answer, one of the men smashed a whiskey bottle on O'Dell's head. He dropped without a quiver, and the crowd roared with approval and shouts of laughter.

Somebody shouted, "Let's send this street sweepings back to New York. We don't need woman-beaters out here."

Another man said thoughtfully, "Let's see, men. First, we got to figure how to get him out the door."

After a chorus of agreement, eager hands lifted O'Dell from the floor. A roaring count of one, two, three followed, and O'Dell flew through the air. When he smashed against the wall beside the door with an impact that shook the building, one of the men said ruefully, "Uh oh, we missed. We better try again."

I turned to Cotton and asked, "Think you can make it back to the hotel?"

He nodded. "I think so, Rube."

"LaRue, I'm sorry about all this."

"Not your fault, Judge. Fact is, you made everything right. I thank you."

O'Dell crashed against the wall again to a mixture of cheers, groans of disappointment, and chants of "Try again. Try again."

"If you pack a little snow in a cloth and put it on that cheek, it'll stop the swelling, ma'am."

She grinned, picked up my coat, and held it for me. After I shrugged it on, she patted my shoulder, stuffed my string tie into a pocket, and said, "You might try the same, Judge. Your face looks crooked."

Jed handed me my Navy, and I asked, "How about a free ride to the hotel?"

He shifted his cud of tobacco and thought it over. "One dollar. You already had a free ride coming here."

O'Dell met the wall and shook the building again.

Cotton, settling his derringers under his coat, said, "One dollar is fine, Jed. I'll treat. Lend me a dollar, will you, Rube?"

LaRue looked over her shoulder and asked, "Should I let them keep doing that, Judge? They'll kill that man right here in my place."

"No, ma'am, I guess not. Ladies forever like to keep order. My mama never let me and my brothers play rough in the house. She always feared we'd break something."

Her piercing whistle cut cleanly through the shouts and laughter. She pointed at the door and said, "Out."

O'Dell's course finally received the necessary correction. On the next attempt, he sailed cleanly until his limp form met the crusted ice at the edge of the street. I chuckled at my own inner joke. Surely, he'd never expected to live up to his name by sailing through the door of a saloon in Wyoming.

The saloon emptied as the crowd followed Sailor outside. Betting started about how many throws it would take to get him to the railroad station.

TWENTY-FOUR

JED SPAT and slapped the reins to start his patient team moving.

Cotton asked, "Isn't the hotel back the other way?"

"Yeah. I figured you and the Judge might want to wander past Doc Jordan's. He might clean you up some before your women see you."

Cotton settled back and kept quiet after that. After Jordan stitched and bandaged my cheek and pronounced that Cotton just had bruises and, maybe, a mild concussion, Jed took us down past the general store. When he drew up in front, Cotton stared at me and made a straight mouth. I stubbornly sat mute and waited him out. Finally, he gave up, bit the bullet, and asked the dumb question. "All right, why did you bring us here?"

Jed sniffed, rolled his chew, and spat. "Water bottles. You need something to pack snow in to ease the swelling. Otherwise you'll both start a panic. Folks'll think we got leprosy in town."

Cotton sat like a stone, showing every sign he'd sit there until spring. He held a hand over his bruised face and hardened into a statue. Feeling like a circus clown, I groaned and went inside, bloody shirt, battered and bandaged face, and all. I endured curious stares as stoically as I could manage and got out again as quick as I could.

Jed chuckled and tempted me to break his neck when he said, "You're going to be a handsome bridegroom. Nice white bandage like that ought to look great in a wedding, matching up with the bride's dress and all that." The more he thought about it, the more he enjoyed his own sorry joke. But he couldn't leave it alone. He had to add in a prissy voice, "The white makes such a fetching contrast with the black and blue basic color." He snickered all the way back to the hotel.

When he stopped the team in front, I asked, "Jed, what's your last name?"

He said, "Just call me Jed. That's good enough."

I got down and grabbed the reins. Something told me I'd found a way to stop his cackling and sniggering. "No. I want to know your whole name."

Cotton climbed down like a sick man of ninety. "Yeah, I'd like to know too, Jed. What is it?"

Jed muttered, "Swmmmmmm."

I leaned forward. "What? What was that? I didn't hear you."

Cotton stepped closer. "Me neither. What did you say?"

Jed jerked the reins and said gruffly, "Turn me loose. I got work to do. I got to make a living."

"Come on, Jed. What's your name?" I had the smell of blood now. I held his reins in an iron grip.

He leaned far over and whispered, "Sweetlace."

Cotton, bruised face rigidly under control, asked, "What was that? Sweetplace?"

"No," I said quickly. "It was Sweetface, wasn't it?"

Cotton said, "Sweetbase? Was it Sweetbase?"

Jed jerked on the reins again, so I released them. He said grimly, "You call me anything but Jed, and I'll go buy a gun." He drove off with a clatter.

Cotton watched him round a corner on two wheels and said, "Can you imagine the teasing he must have taken when he was a boy?"

"Can you imagine what he's going to get if he laughs at us again? That old man's been spurring me at every jump ever since I hit town."

We had a good chuckle until we walked into the hotel lobby. Helen and Nancy sat waiting for us. Both came to their feet with horrified expressions. Nancy stood with one hand covering her mouth but had nothing to say for once.

Helen, wide-eyed, spoke. "You want to tell us about it, or should we just sit down and cry with you?"

Cotton said, "Sitting down sounds good. Let's make the cook give us some coffee."

We told the story. When we finished, Helen asked, "How many men are you going to shoot before you get this out of your system?"

Cotton protested, "Not fair, Helen. The man intended to kill Luke."

Nancy said, "I thought you were face down on the floor when that happened, O great warrior. How would you know?"

"Never mind, O sarcastic maiden, I was just resting a minute. Besides, I heard the man say so himself before he died."

I knew I wasn't in bad trouble when Helen leaned forward and said, "Love your eye. It's turning all kinds of pretty colors. Can you see anything out of that little crack?"

Nancy jumped up, grabbed my package from the general store, and said, "Let's go find some clean snow, Helen. We'll play cold face with these two." She threw a glance at me. "You might want to change shirts, Luke. That bloody thing makes me gag."

I came to my feet to give her a courtly bow. "Thank you, Miss Aldro. You always have something sweet to say."

They put on coats and went on a snow hunt. Cotton looked solemnly at me and said, "Do you keep finding new sore places?"

"Yeah."

"They must have knocked me out and then tap-danced on me. I'm sore everywhere."

"Yeah."

"I never had a fist fight before. Do you always get this sore?"

"Yeah."

"God, how I love conversations with you, Rube. Sheer excitement. Peerless stimulation."

"You want excitement? Take a casual look out the window. Tell me if you see two tall, dark, long-haired men in leather and furs."

Cotton shifted in his chair, the picture of a man making himself comfortable, and his gaze swept across the front windows. He sighed. "This is turning into a hell of a day."

"Somebody in the Dorcas family is clever. Two boys ride into town. They pop a cap, make a big smoke, and run. If they get one of us, good. If they don't, good. Either way they pull the marshal out of town. They circle back, and they always find us right here in the hotel. We're making this too easy for them. It's getting late. It'll be dark soon. They'll do their work and ride away fast. They'll get a full night's ride for a lead on anybody who tries to follow. I like it."

"I hate it. What do we do, Rube?"

"We meet them head on. I see only one problem. Where's the third one?"

"Yeah, how do we find him?"

"Where would you like to be if you were the third Dorcas, Cotton?"

He rubbed his nose for a second or two. "Behind, or off well to one side to make us turn to shoot."

"Sounds practical. Another thing, how do you suppose they intend to draw us out of the hotel?"

"How about the simple and direct way, just yell a challenge?"

I shrugged. "Why not? It's about time I found something simple in my life. Those boys are riflemen. They'll stay clear over on the other side of the street as far from us as they can get. How good are you at long shots with a pistol, Cotton?"

He lifted his coffee, found it cold, and made a wry face. "I'm sorry you asked. At a time like this, I need to be more honest than modest. It's kind of embarrassing just to say it right out, but I think I'm the best there is, Rube. I've burned my weight in powder at long targets."

"Shooting at men is different."

His gaze never wavered. "I didn't find it so when a couple of so-called men tried to bother Helen one time. I went to a lot of trouble to preserve her spotless and aristocratic virtue for an unappreciative rake like you."

My mind flew back to my first visit to Chance Lorane's office. I'd forgotten Chance's conversation. My remark hadn't been smart. I must have sounded like a condescending ass. "No offense intended, Cotton."

He shifted in his chair to turn away from the window and drew his revolver. Carefully examining each load, he said, "I'm deeply offended. I don't think our friendship can survive the hurt I feel."

A slight, strikingly handsome man wearing a short Spanish jacket ambled across the street. A bone-white scar marked his right cheek, somehow heightening his good looks. He spoke briefly to another man who towered over him. Tall, lean, and dark, the second man wore what looked like a permanent, cynical smile.

I couldn't keep the excitement from my voice. "We've got help, Cotton, big help. Next time you look, take note of the pretty little dandy in the Spanish jacket. That's Ward. Then find the tall Indian-looking man with the irritating grin. That's Milt. They're my brothers. One of them all by himself would outnumber the Dorcas family."

"End of surprise, Rube. Helen wired them to keep it a secret that they were coming. She figured you'd be thrilled to tears when they walked in at the wedding. They know about the trouble too. Your future wife doesn't keep your secrets worth a damn. Your daddy and his partner, Thackery, they're around town somewhere too. I'll bet Helen ran over to where they've been hiding from you and told them about the ruckus this afternoon. The Baynes family has its guard up."

"You know them all?"

"Met them every one."

"Good. I'd hate it if you shot at one of my kin by accident. They'd just shoot back and apologize later at your funeral."

"Rube, you get more cheerful by the day. I can't stop laughing around you. Ouch, I just found another sore place." He rubbed his hands together, warming and loosening the fingers.

I pulled my Navy under the table and loaded the sixth chamber. Then I cocked the weapon and held it in my lap. "We go straight at them, Cotton. No hesitating. We walk out the door, walk fast, and get as close as we can before the shooting starts. Nothing fancy. We walk out with gun in hand and split up to make them shoot in two directions. You got a preference?"

"I'd like to be on the left."

"Good, I prefer the right. You ready?"

"I've been trying to think of a way to put it off a little longer, but I can't think of a thing. I'm ready. Let's get started."

"Don't walk in a straight line, Cotton. Make it as hard for them as you can."

"I obey, O great wise man."

"Now?"

"Now."

We both rose and walked briskly through the doorway leading to the lobby, turned smartly and jerked open the front door. I went through first and reached the edge of the porch in two strides. Ignoring the steps, I jumped to the ground and took a path angling to the right. My eyes must have rolled in my head like a locoed steer as I tried with all my might to scan every window, every alley, every door. The skin between my shoulder blades crawled in anticipation of a Dorcas bullet from behind me, but I daren't turn.

Both the savage-looking men straightened at the sight of us. Nobody spoke. They hesitated a second or two, and I felt sure our coming at them caught them by surprise. I hoped they weren't quite ready. Then the dark man on my side, on the right, threw his heavy rifle to his shoulder. I beat him, shot him without breaking stride. My bullet caught him an instant before he fired. Flame spewed from the muzzle of the long rifle, an orange blossom in the dusk. The strike of my bullet and the recoil of his rifle at almost the same time unbalanced him. He went back two steps before he caught himself.

A quick glance to the left told me that Cotton's man was down, but he lifted a pistol, so I sent a shot at him. My man produced a pistol from somewhere too. Quick. He was quicker than I'd thought he'd be. He fired twice before I could pop another cap, but I felt no hit while I aimed deliberately, still walking fast. My Navy misfired. No help for it. I snapped the hammer back again and brought the Navy into line. Something hit me a paralyzing blow under the heart.

The hit almost knocked the Navy from my hand. When I tightened my grip frantically to keep from dropping it, I fired an accidental shot. Only God knew where that went. I cocked again and brought the barrel down smoothly. My man must have fired his pistol empty. His hands worked frantically to replace his empty cylinder with a fresh one. I had to hurry. The hit had driven the breath from me, and I felt a queer, creeping numbness. My vision was going fuzzy. The blaze of powder from the Navy flashed in my eyes and hid my man. I kept blinking hard and trying, but I couldn't find him. I'd lost my man.

My knees hit the icy ruts, and the Navy fell away somewhere. I couldn't breathe. I dropped forward to rest on my hands and knees, desperately, wildly trying to get some air. Pain drove a sword into my chest. It hurt so awful bad I tried to groan, but I had no air. The icy mud of the street felt sharp and cold against my face when my arms gave way.

Then I got a little air, just a little. The frigid little gasp cost me another sword thrust, but I gave thanks for it. I tried again and suddenly my paralyzed lungs started to function again. Grateful as I was to breathe at all, it hurt so bad I had to groan with every breath. My whole left side felt numb. Even my arm felt like it had gone to sleep, but it worked. I shoved myself back up to my hands and knees somehow, and I found my Navy almost under my nose. I picked it up and cocked it.

Strength came flowing back into me. Breathing that hurts is still breathing. Grunting with each breath, I crawled forward for awhile before I thought my legs had a chance to support me. The light grew paler, the sun already down, but my eyes seemed clear. Still, I couldn't find my man. I'd offer my fortune for a post to grab, anything to help me to my feet, but nobody puts posts in the middle of streets. I fought to my feet, groaning between clenched teeth, and I found my man. He lay still, on his back, right where he should be. One wooden-legged step at a time, I dragged forward until I finally stood over him, a man I'd killed but never even spoken to.

Still groggy, I turned carefully, worried that if I stumbled I'd fall, and if I fell, I'd never rise. Cotton stood in the middle of the street. He shouted, "Rube! Can't you hear me?"

"Sure, I hear you."

"I saw you down, and you wouldn't answer me. Scared me to death. You all right?"

"I'm hit hard, Cotton. I'm hit near the center. Why're you standing out in the middle of the street?"

"Can't move. I took one in both legs. If I try to move, I know I'll fall down. I'm scared if I fall down I'll die. I guess I'll stand here till I leaf out in the spring."

The pain in my chest eased, and I found I could straighten to my full height. "I'll come help you."

"You're hit worse than I am, aren't you?"

"Maybe, but I feel all right. Here I come." I found I could walk pretty good. I got to him without hurting myself. Both his trouser legs showed a bright stain.

"Put your arm across my shoulders. We'll head back to the hotel."

"Hell, Rube, I can't reach up there. I'd need a ladder."

A slight form appeared beside us. "Use me. I'm short too."

"Hello, Ward. You're a real Californio. Neat jacket."

"Hello, Luke." Ward stepped close and put his arms around me. He just held on for about five seconds, face pressed against my chest. Nobody said anything. Then he stepped away as if nothing had happened. That kid always pulled tears from my eyes when he did that. Every single time, it got to me.

My pa and Thackery, his partner, stood on the hotel porch, both unmoving, pistols in hand at their sides. Nancy and Helen ran out in the street to us. Helen grabbed my arm with a grip so fierce I gritted my teeth. I could feel her trembling like a struck banjo string. Nancy just stared at Cotton like she wanted to pick him up and run off to a safe place. Neither of the women said a word. Milt's wife, Cris, fiery hair brightening the dark porch, stood close beside my pa. Ward's wife, Kit, large with child, stood beside Thackery, one hand on her daddy's shoulder.

The crowd of us, all so close together, made me nervy. "Be careful, Ward. There were supposed to be three of them. Cotton and I only got two. I don't know where the other one is."

"There were four, Luke. A city man bought in. I don't know what his stake in the game was. I got the other Dorcas when he stepped out from the alley beside the hotel. Milt, hanging back like he always does, saw the city man."

Cotton asked, "Did the city man get away?"

Ward's eyebrows rose an inch. "Get away? From Milt?"

I asked, "Where's Milt now?"

"Staring at bodies. You know how suspicious he is. He's making sure nobody's faking."

Milt spoke from behind us. "Nobody's faking. They're all honest men. Who the hell is Pellham Solder? I found a letter to him on that city man who tried to shoot at you, Luke."

Cotton said, "He's the one causing all the trouble."

Milt said, "He's reformed." He put his hand on my shoulder. "Saw you fall, Luke. Where you hit?"

"Dead center, or nearly so. I don't feel any blood though. Is that a bad sign?"

He pulled my coat open, first one side, then the other. "No blood. Where does it hurt?"

"Right here." I didn't have the courage to look.

Our slow progress toward the hotel ceased. Everybody stopped and turned to stare at me, waiting for Milt to say something.

Milt fumbled around with my coat for another second or two and then said, "Here it is. I found it. You've been shot square in the Gospel, Luke." He held out my new Bible, a hole in one side but none in the other. "We'll wait till we get up to a better light. You can open the Book to find out what page the bullet stopped on. Might be a message for you. I bet you've got a rib or two broken though."

Jed pulled up beside us. "Need an ambulance?"

Ward raised a brow at me.

"Would you go with Cotton and Nancy to the doctor, Ward? Jed's a friend. He knows where the doctor lives. Jed, this is my brother Ward."

Jed said, "One dollar for each passenger."

I asked, "Is that your sweetest price?"

Jed said, "One dollar for the bunch."

"Pay Jed, will you, Ward? Cotton's broke."

EPILOGUE

THE BAYNES WOMEN fell in love with my Helen. No matter how fiercely independent a man may feel, that's a blessing in a close family like mine.

Our women took to Nancy too. Came all the way back to Wyoming for her wedding the next summer, Ward's Kit carrying a new Baynes in her arms, Milt's Cris getting big with another Baynes on the way. Cotton's legs healed just fine several months before the wedding, but it was still too late for him. He was past running by the time his legs were up to it.

Nancy kept my Navy. Named her first-born Luke. Good trade.

Bobby Nels became Aldro's foreman at age twenty. Born cattleman.

I never opened that Bible. Some mysteries are best left undisturbed. Helen gave me a new one.

JOHN S. MCCORD is a retired lieutenant colonel in the U.S. Army. His Double D Western debut, *Walking Hawk*, was a finalist for both the Western Writers of America Spur Award for Best Western of 1989 and their Medicine Pipe Bearer Award for Best First Novel. The previous books in the Baynes clan trilogy are *Montana Horseman* and *Texas Comebacker*. John S. McCord lives with his wife, Joan, in Bedford, Texas, where they are both members of the Dallas/Fort Worth Writers' Workshop.